# Acclaim for the Work
## of DONALD

"Brilliant."
—*GQ*

"A wonderful read."
—*Playboy*

"Marvelous."
—*Entertainment Weekly*

"Dark and delicious."
—*New York Times*

"Westlake is a national literary treasure."
—*Booklist*

"Westlake knows precisely how to grab a reader, draw him or her into the story, and then slowly tighten his grip until escape is impossible."
—*Washington Post Book World*

"Tantalizing."
—*Wall Street Journal*

"A brilliant invention."
—*New York Review of Books*

"A tremendously skillful, smart writer."
—*Time Out New York*

"The wildest, screwiest, fastest-paced yet…It is also insanely funny."
—*Des Moines Register*

I switched on the TV, settling down to watch the local news. You don't really get local news in New York, because New York is too big. For an automobile accident, say, to make it on New York's local news, it has to have taken place on the George Washington Bridge at rush hour, between a truckload of dynamite and a car driven by fleeing terrorists who've just kidnapped the Israeli ambassador. And sunk the bridge. In the sticks, for an automobile to make the TV news, all it has to do is hit something. Anything. A fire hydrant will do.

There came a knock at the door. It was Katharine. She looked slightly worried, but trying to hide it, and she said, "Barry would like to talk to you."

I followed her across the hall. I picked up the receiver. "Hello?"

"Is that the driver?" He sounded less pleasant than when I'd overheard him before.

"That's right," I said.

"I've been following your route here, Fletcher," he said, "and it doesn't seem to me you're coming out the quickest way."

"Oh, no?"

"I don't get it," he said. "I don't understand what you're doing on Route 70. You taking her for a ride, Fletcher? You want to see Vegas at somebody else's expense?"

"You work out the mileage, Mac," I told him. "And then I tell you what you do. You don't do any cab driving, and I don't do any face changing. Here's your intended." And I handed the phone to Katharine, saying, "If I was on my way to marry that guy, I'd go by tricycle..."

# Call ME a CAB

## by **Donald E. Westlake**

A HARD CASE CRIME NOVEL

**A HARD CASE CRIME BOOK**
(HCC-152)
*First Hard Case Crime edition: February 2022*

Published by

Titan Books
A division of Titan Publishing Group Ltd
144 Southwark Street
London SE1 0UP

in collaboration with Winterfall LLC

Print edition ISBN 978-1-78909-818-1
E-book ISBN 978-1-78909-820-4

Design direction by Max Phillips
*www.maxphillips.net*

Typeset by Swordsmith Productions

The name "Hard Case Crime" and the Hard Case Crime logo are trademarks of Winterfall LLC. Hard Case Crime books are selected and edited by Charles Ardai.

Printed and bound by CPI Group (UK) Ltd, Croydon CR0 4YY

*Visit us on the web at www.HardCaseCrime.com*

*For Abby—fellow traveler*

*To travel hopefully is a better thing than to arrive.*
ROBERT LOUIS STEVENSON

She hailed me on East 62nd Street, not far from Bloomingdale's. She was an attractive girl, wearing big-lensed sunglasses against the June glare, and carrying two plaid suitcases, one of which she waggled at me as I rolled down the street. "Say 'Kennedy,' " I whispered, and eased the cab to a stop.

Opening the rear door, she shoved the suitcases in first, then followed, slammed the door, shoved the sunglasses up on top of her head, and said, "Kennedy."

"You got it," I said, and started the meter with a smile. Not only is the long expensive run from Manhattan out to John F. Kennedy International Airport in Queens one of the joys of a cabby's life, but there's no pleasanter way to drive anywhere than with a good-looking woman in the rearview mirror.

Unless, of course, she's crazy. And in this instance the early signs were not good. This girl did not sit back in the seat as I started off, nor did she cross her legs and look out at the passing world, nor did she take a compact from her shoulder bag so she could study the present condition of her face; all the normal things a good-looking young woman does when settling down alone for a long cab ride. What she *did* do was talk to herself, muttering phrases I couldn't quite hear. And she kept putting her hands up to both sides of her face like the blinkers on a horse, running her fingers through her long brown hair and then tossing the hair backward in a heavy double wave. And she frowned a lot, and made strange unpleasant faces, and stared at the floor or at the back of my neck. And sat forward on the seat, very tense and upset.

Part of the reason this behavior discomfited me was the lack of a safety partition between the back of my head and the passenger space. In New York City, all the major-company cabs are required to install that safety partition, but the law says private cab owners can decide for themselves, and the private owner of this particular Checker (who just happened to be my own father) had decided not to go the expense. Normally I like it that way, preferring the increased opportunity for friendly conversation and other human contact, but human contact with a crazy person is where I draw the line.

I endured it all the way down Second Avenue and through the Midtown Tunnel, but after I'd paid the toll and accelerated up to speed on the Expressway and she *still* hadn't settled down I felt I had to do or say something to alter the situation. Frankly, she was making me nervous. So I looked in the mirror and I called, "Excuse me!"

She flashed a quick, irritable, distracted look. "What?"

I said, "You a jumper?"

At least I had her attention. *"What?"*

"Friend of mine had one in his cab," I explained. "A suicide, you know? She wanted to jump off a building, but she was afraid of heights."

She was staring now like Medusa. "A *suicide?*"

That was the wrong subject. "Afraid of heights," I corrected her. "Try to keep up, will you? This girl's idea was, she could get the same effect if she jumped out of a cab doing sixty."

*"I'm* not a suicide," she said. And it was true she now looked more outraged than despondent.

"That's good," I said, "because it won't work. There's too much air pressure against the door at this speed, you couldn't get it open."

She glanced at the door, then rather angrily at me. "I'm not a suicide," she repeated.

"Fine."

After that she settled back in the seat at last, obviously thinking things over, and I concentrated on the traffic until she herself picked up the conversation, out past the cemeteries, telling me, "I just have a decision to make, that's all."

So I gave her my philosophy, in a nutshell. "Don't do it."

"Don't do what?"

"Don't make decisions. They can only cause trouble."

"But I promised," she said. "And I always keep my promises. Always."

"Then don't make promises."

She smiled, a bit ruefully; meaning, it's too late not to make this particular promise. Well, it wasn't too late to break it, but who am I to lead another person out of confusion and into the light? I kept my advice to myself, and once again the conversation lapsed.

And once again she was the one to pick it up, just as I made the transfer from the Expressway to the Van Wyck, saying as though there hadn't been any pause at all, "It's about getting married."

"Married?" I don't believe in marriage. "Good luck," I said, and some irony may have crept into my voice.

"It isn't right," she said. "I just keep turning the poor guy down."

"Maybe he's the wrong guy."

"He's the *right* guy," she insisted. "He's sweet and understanding, he's handsome and rich, he loves me and I love him— what more could I possibly want?"

"Thursdays off?"

"I don't know *what* I want," she said, shaking her head. "It's just such a big decision, that's all."

"Mm hm." I'd already given my advice on decisions.

"For two years I've been trying to marry him," she said. "That poor guy, I've left him waiting at the marriage license bureau, at the church, and on the JP's front porch."

"He puts up with a lot."

"He's *very* understanding. That's why I love him so much. But now he says he can't wait anymore."

"Oh, yeah?"

"He says he wants to marry *me*, but he says he also just wants to get *married*."

"Determined fella."

"So I promised him, faithfully, just now on the phone, I'm coming out to Los Angeles—"

"That's where he is, huh?"

"And when I get off the plane, I'll either say *yes* or *no*. If it's *yes*, we'll get right in his car and drive straight to Nevada and be married *today*."

"Wow," I said.

"If it's *no*," she said, "he says we'll shake hands and part, and I can take the next plane back to New York."

"So it's do or die. The crunch. Down to the bottom line. This is the nitty gritty."

"That's right," she said. "Five hours from now I'll be in Los Angeles, and I have to be *sure* by then." She shook her head fiercely, agitating her heavy hair. "How can a person make a decision for their whole life in five hours?"

"I don't know," I said. "With me the question has never come up."

And once more the conversation waned, as she settled back in the seat, biting on the knuckle of her right thumb and brooding about this crisis point in her life. I continued to drive, she continued to brood, and then I became aware that she was staring at the back of my neck; fixedly, the way I imagine a vampire would. I was beginning to get nervous again when she called out: "Say."

"Yeah?"

"This sign here," she said. "Ask Driver For Out Of Town Rates."

Ah; that was the notice glued to the back of my headrest, so it wasn't my throat she'd been studying after all. I said, "Yeah?"

And she said, "How much to Los Angeles?"

"A hundred million dollars," I said.

"No, I mean it," she said.

She couldn't possibly mean it. A little annoyed, I said, "Come on, Miss."

"Listen, umm—" she said, and leaned forward to look at the license mounted in front of the glove compartment. She wanted my name. "Thomas," she said. "Listen, Thomas, I'm serious. I told Barry I'd make up my mind by the time I got to Los Angeles, and I *promised* him I'd leave today, but I just can't do it in five hours. How long would it take to drive there? Five or six days?"

I was reluctant to be in this conversation at all. "Probably," I said.

Her expression became almost dreamy. "Away from all distractions," she said. "Away from the office, just driving, plenty of time to think. By the time we got there I'd *know*, I'd be sure of myself."

It was time to bring her down from the clouds, so she could catch her plane. "It'd be goddam expensive," I said.

"How much?"

"You want me to find out?"

"Yes, please."

So I switched on the two-way radio. We belong to one of the radio-dispatch outfits—Speediphone Cabs—but unless a fare leaves me in some outlandish backwater I prefer to cruise and find my customers on the street. The kind of people who phone for a cab instead of going outside and hailing one usually live in outlandish backwaters themselves, where there aren't any cabs to hail. In any event, the radio had been off, but now I switched it on, and immediately the cab filled with the harsh voice of Hilda The Dispatcher: "...to Madison and 35th. One-eight."

Pressing the button on its side, I spoke into my mike, giving my call number: "Two-seven."

"One-eight," Hilda insisted, that being the guy she'd decided to talk to next.

Phooey. "Two-seven!" I said, more forcefully.

"One-eight!" she said, *much* more forcefully.

So I tried tact. "I'll be one-eight if you want me to be one-eight, Hilda," I said, "but I'm really two-seven."

"Tom? Get off, I'm trying to talk to one-eight."

"But I'm ready to talk *now*."

Hilda's sigh came across the airwaves like static. "All right, Tom," she said. "What is it?"

"I got an out of town, she wants a price."

"Where to?"

"Los Angeles," I said.

There was a little silence, and then Hilda said, "One-eight!"

"Listen, Hilda," I said, "this is on the level."

"A cab to Los Angeles?" She remained dubious, for which I could hardly blame her.

"That's right," I said. "The customer's in the cab, she wants a price."

"Jesus," Hilda said. "Shut up, one-eight, I got a problem. Tom? I'll get back to you."

"Right," I said, cradled the microphone, and turned the receiver volume down to where I could barely hear it.

The passenger said, "Shouldn't we head the other way now?"

Were we really going to Los Angeles? So far everything was still on the meter, so it didn't matter where we went. "Sure," I said.

We were at that moment arriving at the junction of the Van Wyck and the Belt Parkway, just before the airport, and we did a sweep-around of rare and singular beauty, hardly slowing down at all. I took the second Parkway exit (northbound), looping down and to the right away from the Van Wyck like a fighter plane peeling off in a World War Two movie, then swept around onto the Belt, ran under the Van Wyck, took the next exit curving up and to the right, came out onto the Van Wyck in the opposite direction, and laid out toward Manhattan.

The passenger was very excited. She kept looking out the rear window, as though to see the plane she wasn't catching, and she kept saying things like, "It's the only way. It's the only thing that makes sense. I can be *sure* of myself. Barry will understand." That last part was said with a little less excitement and conviction, but she quickly rallied and repeated some of the other sentences some more.

It was perhaps eight minutes before the intermittent tiny squawking of the radio squawked my call number, and then I turned up the receiver volume, grabbed the mike, and said, "Right here."

"Four thousand dollars," Hilda said. "Plus your expenses." Her tone of voice said, *There. Now leave me alone with all this nonsense.*

I looked in the rearview mirror. "Did you hear it?"

"Four thousand dollars." She'd heard it, all right; she was pale and worried. "I *have* that much," she said, more to herself than me. "In my savings account, for income tax. I could stall, just pay the interest—" She frowned and chewed her lower lip, working it out, while I drove not too rapidly westward. Then all at once she sat up straighter, her expression full of determination, and said, "Yes."

"You're sure?"

"It's worth it," she said. "For peace of mind, the rest of my life? It's cheap. The IRS can wait."

"Okay." Into the mike I said, "She says it's a go. Tell my father, will you?"

"Cash, or certified check," Hilda said.

"That's fine," the passenger said. "We'll just stop by my bank, and we'll be on our way."

# 2

Well, of course, it wasn't *quite* that easy. Back in Manhattan we stopped at her bank for the certified check made out to Harry Fletcher (my father), which I mailed to my parents' house in Queens, and then we drove downtown to my apartment on East 17th Street. The passenger waited in the cab while I threw some clothing and a toothbrush into my old canvas bag with all the zippers—given me by my parents when I went away to college—and then I sat down at the dinette table to compose a note to Rita.

About Rita. She was the closest thing I had to an actual girlfriend at that time. She worked for a magazine company on the West Side, and sometimes she'd come downtown and stay with me for a couple of days. She had her own key, some of her clothing and cosmetics lived here, and if she made a long-distance call she always paid up when I got my next bill. "You only want me for my body," I told her once, when she dropped in unannounced and I woke up to find her crawling to bed with me. "Bragging or complaining?" she asked, and I said, "What if I had somebody else here?" She said, "Then I'd tiptoe out again." It wasn't what you could call an intense relationship.

As demonstrated by the note: "Am taking a fare out of town, will be gone a couple weeks, phone you when I get back. Better smell the yogurt before you eat it."

Outside, I put my bag on the front seat and said, "Well, Ms. Scott—" (I knew her name now, Katharine Scott, from the check) "—you still game?"

"Definitely," she said.

"Fine," I said, and took the FDR Drive and the Harlem River Drive up to the George Washington Bridge. All the way up, Ms. Scott sat in the back seat with that alert, scrubbed, determined, brave, optimistic look of someone who's just made an absolutely *right* resolution, and hasn't broken it yet.

Across the bridge into New Jersey, and I followed the signs for Interstate 80, lining out due west into what would have been the setting sun if it wasn't still morning. Switching on my radio one last time, I said, "Two-seven. Two-seven. Two-seven."

"Tom? Is that you?" There was a lot of static in the air. "I can barely hear you."

"We're on our way, Hilda," I said, speaking loud and clear. "The certified check is in the mail, and we just crossed the George Washington Bridge."

"Good luck," she said, through the buzz of static.

"Thanks. See you in a couple weeks."

She said something I couldn't make out, with all the static. I yelled, "What?"

"Your father says don't wreck his cab!"

"Okay, okay," I said. "Tell him don't worry."

"What?"

"I said okay!"

"Okay! Drop us a postcard!"

"I will!" I yelled, and listened to nothing but static for a few seconds, and switched off.

# 3

Pennsylvania. Two P.M., two hundred miles from New York. Route 80, speed 80. Dark green forested mountains massed in brilliant sunshine under a deep blue sky. Weather clear, track fast, passenger asleep.

She'd corked off about five minutes out of New York. She'd been looking around as we'd crossed the bridge, bright and happy, smiling at everything, very up and positive, and all of a sudden she was asleep. Still smiling, but totally unconscious, curled up on the seat with her black cardigan unwrapped from her throat and spread out over her legs.

I knew what that meant; the end of tension. You worry about a problem, and worry and worry, until finally you *do* something, it doesn't matter what, right or wrong, sensible or stupid, and the relief that comes from *action* is so great you just relax right down into sleep.

On the other hand, sooner or later you have to wake up, and I was prepared to bet even money that when Ms. Scott reopened her eyes the first thing she'd say would be, "Take me back to New York!" This cab-to-California idea had been a lunge at decision-making, that's all, just a temporary way to ease the pressure.

Which from my point of view would be a pity; driving to California was okay with *me*. Although I'd been to Los Angeles twice, I'd never seen the country in between. And the driving, while there'd be more of it, would be a lot easier than my usual fifteen hundred city miles per four-day week. Driving the Interstates, in my opinion, is mostly like sitting in the front row at a movie theater during a travelogue. Also, I was comfortable in this cab, it had been my office, my den, my studio apartment for nearly three years. Around the driver's seat, among my father's knickknacks—the cream-colored ex-Saint Christopher statue glued to the dash, for instance, or his World War Two Purple Heart pinned to the top fabric above the visor—were some knickknacks of my own; a laminated picture of me from my high school paper showing me shooting a basket (actually I missed), a counterfeit ten-dollar bill I'd been stuck with about three years ago, other things like that. It was a congenial environment.

On the other hand, starvation was setting in. This might be a wonderful escapade, but I wanted something to eat. Ever since I was five years old I've understood that adventures stop for lunch.

I'd been waiting for my passenger to awaken, but now my stomach had begun to make low growling sounds; any minute it might attack. And up ahead, just beyond that next exit, looking high in the sky on long poles, between similarly tall Exxon and Shell signs, was the familiar giant yellow M of a McDonald's. Fine. I could pop in there, leaving Ms. Scott asleep in the cab, and grab myself some lunch to go.

No sooner said than done. The exit ramp curved around a shaggy green hill to a two-lane blacktop country road. The giant yellow M was off to my left; heading that way, I found at its base a tiny stand that was very anticlimactic. After that huge sign, you'd expect at least the Taj Mahal.

I parked the cab with the three or four other cars in the lot, climbed out, stretched, and realized the men's room took priority ever over lunch. The toilets were around to the side; I went there, came back to the front, and entered the stand. Inside was cool and dim after the bright sunlight. I ordered a

Big Mac, onion rings on the side, a Coke and another Big Mac (I'd decided I was more than usually hungry), and when I carried it all back to the cab the passenger was gone.

What now? I looked around in the bright sunshine, and failed to see her. The Shell station was to the left, the Exxon across the road; other than that, the countryside was unpopulated hilly green forest. A station wagon driven by a woman in curlers and filled with children and food drove by, heading out; my passenger wasn't in it. Nor was she in the other cars parked nearby.

I was turning in my third bewildered circle, my hands still encumbered with little white paper bags full of lunch, when the lady herself came around the corner of the building. Of course; rest stop for everybody. I smiled and gestured with my paper bags, and she smiled back, nodding and pointing at the front entrance to the stand. "Right," I called, and she went inside while I got back behind the wheel.

I could see her through the tinted windows, talking to the high school boy behind the counter. Hmmm. Should I go ahead and eat my lunch, or should I wait for the passenger to come back? What was the etiquette in such a situation?

I decided to wait, and soon enough here she came, with her own collection of white paper bags. I got out and opened the rear door for her, she thanked me, I placed myself behind the wheel again, and she said, "Where are we?"

"Somewhere in wildest Pennsylvania." While talking I was opening my first Big Mac. "According to the speedometer, a little more than two hundred miles from the bridge."

"What bridge?"

"George Washington. When we left New York."

"Oh, of course, I'm sorry. I guess I'm not really awake yet."

I didn't answer until I'd finished chewing and swallowing a

great big bite of Big Mac, washing it down with Coke. Then I said, "You had a good sleep, huh?"

"Wonderful. Best I've had in weeks."

I had to know the answer to the main question, so I asked it: "You still want to go forward?"

"Of course," she said. "Don't you?"

"We are here to serve."

"Besides," she said, "I paid the money."

"Oh, we could work something out on that. You pay my time and gas, and we give you back the rest."

She frowned, thinking it over—I was sitting sideways in the seat, looking at her directly instead of through the mirror—but then she shook her head, made a determined face, and said, "No. It's the right way to do it. I couldn't go back now, catch another plane, call Barry again, I just couldn't go through all that. I've made this decision, I'll stick by it."

"Fine," I said.

"So that's settled. What do I owe you for lunch?"

"Lunch?" I stared at my white paper bags.

"Expenses, remember?" She was being very brisk and businesslike, shoulder bag open in her lap.

"I eat lunch in New York," I pointed out. "Every day."

She seemed doubtful. "Food is an expense."

"Then it's my treat."

"I tell you what," she said. "You can buy your own lunch, but I'll buy you dinner. That's more expensive when you eat out."

"It's a deal," I said, and popped an onion ring in my mouth.

"Oh! You've got onion rings!"

"I bought em in the McDonald's there."

"I love onion rings. It didn't even occur to me. I tell you what," she said. "I'll trade you, a couple onion rings for a couple french fries."

"I'll go get you some onion rings," I offered.

"No, no, don't do that. We'll just trade a couple, okay?"

Then I understood that this was an important moment. If I was standoffish and strict, if I insisted on going back into the stand and buying another package of onion rings, we would be formal with one another the whole trip, whereas what she really wanted was company.

Well, so did I. "Fine," I said, and put my little cardboard barge of onion rings on top of the seat back.

She moved forward then to the bucket seat, put her french fries next to my onion rings, ate an onion ring, said it was super, and we ate companionably for a while. Then she said, "Do you mind if I talk to you about Barry?"

"That's the guy in Los Angeles?"

"It might clear my mind," she said.

"All I know about him so far," I said, "is that he's got a hell of a lot of patience."

"And that it's running out."

"That, too. What's he do for a living?"

"He's, well…" She seemed oddly hesitant, as though she didn't want me to know, or was afraid I might laugh. "He's a surgeon," she said.

"Oh, yeah? That's terrific."

"A plastic surgeon."

"Oh," I said. A vision rose up in my mind: A phony, in a paisley ascot. Deep chahming baritone, overly manly handshake, a little too ruggedly handsome to be true.

The smile she gave me was rueful. "I know," she said. "People always think it's some sort of joke."

So apparently the vision in my mind had showed on my face. "Not at all," I said. "There are plastic surgeons and plastic surgeons. Some of them do wonderful humanitarian work, rebuilding people after terrible accidents and so on."

"And some of them," she said, "do unnecessary cosmetic surgery on idle rich people, making them pretty and charging them a lot of money."

The irony in her voice led me to suspect the worst. I said, "That's your guy, huh?"

"Barry is a cosmetic plastic surgeon," she said, the same way a mother might announce her oldest boy is a hopeless alcoholic; and then she went on just the way the mother would, looking on the bright side: "But he's very sweet, and very honest. He's very very talented, he's done amazing things with big noses and low foreheads and baggy eyes and—"

"Not while I'm eating."

"The point is," she said, "Barry is a truly wonderful, gentle human being, which is why I love him."

There was a question I wanted to ask, but I didn't know how. Also, I was afraid of the answer. Holding an onion ring, I sort of gestured vaguely toward her face, saying, "Did he, uhhh…?"

She didn't get it. "Did he what?"

"You, um…"

"Oh! *My* face? No, he always says my face is one of the few times God did better work than *he* could."

"A very fancy man with a compliment." It was amazing how much I didn't like Barry.

"Let me show you his picture," she said, and opened the locket dangling on her chest. It turned out to be not exactly a locket after all, but a watch, with a photograph inside the lid. She leaned forward, extending the photo over the seatback, and dumped the onion rings and french fries in my lap. "Oh! I'm terribly sorry."

"No problem." There were fewer onion rings left than french fries, I noticed. I quick ate an onion ring, put everything else back in the barges and the barges back on top of the seat, then leaned forward to look at this paragon among men.

Well. It's very annoying when your prejudices aren't confirmed. The guy smiling in the picture—it was just his head, and a blurred section of what might have been bookcase behind him—looked to be my age (31) or a couple of years older, and seemed a very decent sort of chap indeed. She'd used the word 'gentle' and that was exactly what he looked like. Mild-mannered, easygoing, certainly trustworthy; a solid, likable, everyday nice guy. I'd known a whole lot of them in college. I'd even tried to be one myself for a while. "This guy shouldn't be a plastic surgeon," I said. "He should be a vet."

She understood my meaning at once. "He's very tender," she agreed. "He's very sympathetic to the humiliation people feel when they think they have a blemish."

"Okay," I said. I understood that at a level below consciousness I'd been in competition with Barry—an attractive woman creates male competition simply by existing—and now I saw that in any competition at any level Barry would have to come in first. He'd probably even spell better than me. Worst of all, if I ever met him, as I most likely would at the other end of this trip, I'd undoubtedly like him.

"You see what I mean," she said, and turned the picture around to look at it herself. Smiling fondly at the picture, she said, "He's such a wonderful guy. Why do I keep backing away from him?"

"He's got a flaw somewhere."

"He really doesn't. He's Mister Right."

"Then take the plane."

She sighed, shook her head, and closed the locket. Popping an onion ring into her mouth—when was she going to eat some of her french fries?—she said, "We met four years ago, in Houston. I was doing a shopping mall, and he—"

"A what?"

"A shopping mall. I'm a landscape architect."

"Ah," I said.

"You know what that is, don't you?"

"You decide where the trees go."

She gave me the condescending smile of the professional toward the layman. "Something like that. Anyway, I'm attached to a New York firm, but my work is all around the country."

"What's Barry doing in Los Angeles?"

"That's where he lives."

"And after you're married?"

"I'll switch to a West Coast firm." Was there something slightly defiant about the way she said that?

I nodded. "You're the one has to move, huh? Because you're the woman? Whither thou goest, all that?"

"Not at all. Barry is the least sexist of men."

I'd always thought *I* was. "Uh huh," I said.

"It's better for both our careers, that's all," she explained. "There's at *least* as much work for a landscape architect on the West Coast as the East, and I've always traveled and worked all over the country anyway, so I can just as easily be based in Los Angeles as anywhere else. And that's where most of Barry's patients are, so it's better for him. He says New Yorkers don't care what they look like."

"Oh, yeah?"

"Are we out of onion rings?"

"There's still french fries," I suggested. "Or I could go get another order."

"No, I suppose we ought to push on." She sounded reluctant, though there really wasn't much in this McDonald's lot to hold us.

Then she said, "How far do you want to drive at a time? How should we work that?"

"I'll give you a ten-hour day," I said, "same as I work in the city, which includes lunchtime. I started at ten this morning, so I'll drive till eight tonight, and then we'll stop."

"A ten-hour day—isn't that a lot?"

"It's what I'm used to. Ready?"

"Just a second," she said. "Let me just go get one more order of onion rings. For the road." And she hopped out of the cab and loped away. I watched her go, then spent a minute cleaning up all the paper bags and cardboard barges from the seat beside me.

I liked her.

# 4

Six-thirty P.M. Pennsylvania mountains replaced by Ohio industrial parks. Interstate 80 abandoned for Interstate 76, to get a bit further south. The sun, descending dead ahead toward eye level, gradually becoming a nuisance. The passenger brooding in the back.

After lunch, I'd gassed up at the neighboring Exxon station, then climbed back up onto Route 80 and sailed on into the west. Ms. Scott, after sharing with me the additional order of onion rings, had returned to her previous seat, where she'd opened one of her suitcases and brought out from it a slender vinyl attaché case; the kind carried by State Department clerks, computer salesmen, and executive trainees. This, which she opened on her lap, had proved to contain such serious businesslike material as yellow-lined legal pads, ballpoint pens, graph paper, loose-leaf filler books, a cassette recorder, sharpened yellow pencils, and a slide rule.

(I have always envied people who know what a slide rule is for. It's not even the question of how you use it, it's more basic than that; I am convinced there have been moments in my life which would have been made easier if I had been equipped with a handy slide rule and the mastery of its operation, but I'm so ignorant I don't even know which moments those were. *Never* have I said, "Oh, if only I had a slide rule!" though surely there have been times when it was the appropriate thing to say.)

But not at the moment for Ms. Scott. She'd taken from the attaché case only one legal pad and one ballpoint pen, then closed the case on her lap, used it as a desktop, and proceeded to write…think…chew the pen…brood at the passing scenery …write some more…cross out part of what she'd written… start a new sheet…sometimes crumple a sheet and throw it to the floor…sometimes brood a long long time without writing… sometimes write very rapidly for ten or fifteen minutes at a stretch—and thus the time flew by.

For myself, in addition to the driving and the scenery, I too had Ms. Scott's problem to ponder. Granted it was none of my business, I could hardly avoid *thinking* about it. And something about this fellow Barry was bothering her, that much was plain enough. Was it some flaw not yet mentioned—possibly not even consciously understood or recognized by the lady herself—but which subliminally warned her away? Or was she possibly merely skittish? I'd thought that was supposed to be a male problem, that fidgetiness at the brink of marriage, but could that be the crux of it, after all?

Well, I simply didn't have enough information. She herself knew the whole story, yet couldn't resolve the problem. Still, it gave me something to chew on while driving.

Until six-thirty, that is, when all at once she started, nearly dropped the attaché case off her lap, and cried out, "My God! What time is it?"

I keep a watch with an expansion band on the sun visor. Unfortunately, at the moment the visor was down to protect me from the subsiding sun, so I had to flip it up, squint against that yellow glare in my eyes, and finally make out which little hand was where. "Six twenty-five."

"Oh, good God, I never thought! A phone, we have to find a phone!"

"Check," I said.

"I never called Barry! He must have met that plane!"

"Ah hah," I said. "I bet you're right."

"A phone! A phone!"

"At the earliest opportunity," I assured her.

There are no services on the Interstate itself, but they do erect signs telling you what services are available off the highway at each exit, and a few minutes later we came to one of these. "Services Next Exit," it said. "Gas Food Phone Lodging."

Ms. Scott leaned forward to thump the seatback near my right ear. "There! There! It says phone!"

"I see it."

I took the exit, and found the usual cluster of chain operations along the country road; this time, Kentucky Fried Chicken, Chevron and Hess gasolines, and Stuckey's. A phone booth was out by the road in front of the Chevron station, so I parked the cab next to it.

Ms. Scott had been pawing through her bag, and now she said, "I'm sure I don't have enough change. Do you have change? I *can't* call him collect, not like this."

"Sure," I said. I unhooked my change machine from under the dashboard and handed it back. "Just take this with you."

"I'm sorry," she said, "I've never operated one of those."

I could see this phone-call business was making her very nervous, so I said, "I'll come along, and just hand you change as you need it."

"Good."

We got out of the cab, and then I realized this wasn't an enclosed phone booth, but one of those cockpit-on-a-stick things that offer no privacy. "I'll just give you a lot of change," I said, "and let you alone."

But she wouldn't hear of it. "No no no, it's all right, I just want to tell him what happened, that's all. Stay right here with me, I'm feeling very panicky and stupid, I'd just spill change all over the place."

"Okay."

So she made the call, and the operator told her how much money, and I just kept handing over quarters for a while, which she kept putting into the quarter slot—*bong bong bong*. Then she spoke with the operator again, and said to me, "Fifteen cents more," so I gave her a dime—*bing bing*—and a nickel—*bing*—and at last the call went through.

I suppose they must have turned the volume up on that phone because it was so close to a road; or maybe it was set wrong. Whatever the reason, it turned out I could hear every word, which I found quite embarrassing. Twice I started to tiptoe back toward the cab, but both times Ms. Scott gestured at me strongly to stay where I was. So I stayed, and this is what I heard:

"Hello?" (Ordinary male voice.)

"Hello, sweetheart?"

"*Sweet*-heart!" (*Loud* male voice.)

Ms. Scott was looking very agitated and guilty and upset. "Barry," she said. "It's me. Katharine."

"I remember you." (Annoyed male voice.) "And this time you left me at the airport."

She shook her head. "I'm sorry."

"I thought you always keep your promises."

She was holding the phone in both hands, very intensely. "I *do*," she said.

"You *promised* you'd come to L.A."

"I am. I'm on my way."

"On your *way*? Where are you?"

"Near Akron, Ohio."

"Akro— How are you coming, by *cab*?"

Ms. Scott opened her mouth, but no words came, and she looked over at me with such a bewildered, bedeviled—and at the same time comical—expression on her face that I had to put my hand over my own mouth and turn my head away.

The exasperated voice spoke from the phone: "Hello?"

Ms. Scott sighed. "Yes," she said.

"What?"

"Yes."

"Yes *what*?"

"Yes I'm coming by cab." Then, very emphatically, as though this were an extremely important point she was making and she wanted to be sure he understood its implications, she repeated it: "I am coming by cab."

"I don't believe it," said the voice from the phone. "Or, wait a minute. Yes, I do."

(This was the first time I started to tiptoe away.)

"Barry," she said, earnest and intent, at the same time waving at me to stay, "I was on my way to the airport and I just knew I couldn't do it. I couldn't make up my mind that fast."

"*Fast!*"

"Five hours. Barry, I've spent all day sitting in the cab just *thinking*, and already I'm sure I'm right."

"About what?"

"About taking the cab. It gives me a chance to think, to be alone, no pressures, no distractions. By the time I get to Los Angeles, I'll be sure about everything. I'll know my own mind."

"How long before you get here?"

"The driver tells me it'll be about a week," she said, with a lifted querying eyebrow in my direction. (I nodded.) "Probably next Wednesday."

"The driver?" (*Suspicious* male voice.) "A male driver?"

"Yes." (Innocent female voice.) "Why?"

"What's he like?"

"He's just a cabdriver," Ms. Scott said, waving me back again as for the second time I tried unobtrusively to creep away. "You know what cabdrivers are like."

In my head appeared the image that I knew was now appearing in Barry's head, twenty-five hundred miles away: a short, fat, fiftyish, big-nosed cabdriver in a cloth cap, smoking a cigar.

"All right," said Barry, and why not?

Ms. Scott became intense again: "You don't want to marry me if I'm not *sure*, do you?"

A hell of a question. "I suppose not," said Barry.

"Let me be completely certain in my own mind," she said, "and then I'll be ready."

Barry's sigh rustled down the phone lines. "Well, honey," he said, "anybody who'll take a cab from New York to Los Angeles, I just have to believe you're serious, you really do need this extra time."

"I *knew* you'd understand."

"I don't understand. I'm going along with it, but I don't even begin to understand. But you'll phone me every day?"

"Oh, of *course*."

"And you're coming directly to Los Angeles. No side trips."

"Directly."

"And you'll be here next Wednesday."

"No later. I promise. And you know I always keep my promises."

"Yee-ess."

"I *do* love you, Barry."

"And I must love you, Katharine," said the long-suffering voice.

"Goodbye, sweetheart. Phone you tomorrow."

"Right. Right."

Ms. Scott hung up, sighed a long sigh, and looked over at me. "There," she said. "Do you see what I mean?"

"Yeah," I said. "I'm afraid I do."

# 5

At five past eight, when I saw the Holiday Inn sign far ahead, high in the evening sky like a tacky UFO, we were still in Ohio, now on Interstate 70, but Indiana was very close.

On the other hand, I was very weary. Highway driving is less physically demanding than city driving, but it's also more monotonous and thus finally more tiring. We'd made three stops—lunch & gas, phone & gas, and gas—but otherwise I'd just been sitting here all day while Ms. Scott brooded in the back, and now I was ready for something else. Indiana could wait.

"Holiday Inn ahead," I called.

"What? Where?"

She must have been *really* involved in her own thoughts not to see that monster in the sky. "Up there," I said. "It's a little after eight, we ought to stop."

"Oh. Okay, fine."

I took the exit, swung right on the county road, and turned in at the Holiday Inn just past the Sohio station. We left the cab together and walked into the lobby, a long low-ceilinged room with purple-and-maroon carpeting and drapes and wall fabric, plus a lot of Revolutionary War wall plaques. The place was air-conditioned down to about eleven degrees Fahrenheit. I hung back to let Ms. Scott make the arrangements, but the desk clerk in his yellow sport jacket looked past her at me, smiled, and said, "Good evening."

"Good evening," I said.

Ms. Scott said, "We'd like rooms for tonight."

The desk clerk flickered his smile at her, then back at me, then back at her again. Speaking more or less to the space between us, he said, "Oh, yes? Just for the one night?"

I kept myself from nodding, and Ms. Scott said, "That's right."

"A double?"

"Two singles," she said.

"Connecting?"

The guy was becoming, in my personal opinion, a pain in the ass, but Ms. Scott remained calm and businesslike. "That won't be necessary," she said.

"That's fine, then." And, turning to *me*, he said, "Will you be paying with a credit card, sir?"

"American Express," said the calm voice to my left. How she maintained her cool I don't know, but without the slightest hint of annoyance Ms. Scott removed a wallet from her shoulder bag, a credit card from the wallet, and placed the card on the counter.

"Fine, fine, fine," the desk clerk said. He had clearly decided he didn't like us, because we were confusing him. Picking up the credit card, he placed two registration forms on the counter in its place and said, "If you'll just fill these out. Thank you." And turned away to consult charts and graphs, and to play with his credit card machine.

Ms. Scott and I had just started filling in our forms when a very embarrassed-looking man in a red robe with dragons writhing on it, plus old scuff slippers on his feet, approached the desk. "Excuse me," he said.

A couple who were a couple would automatically have moved a bit to one side for this interruption. Ms. Scott and I automatically moved a bit further apart, so the man in the robe had no choice but to stand between us for his dealings with the desk clerk, who turned back from his credit card machine to say, "Sir?"

The man in the robe was *horribly* embarrassed. "I'm terribly sorry," he said, and while his strained eyes looked straight ahead at the desk clerk his cheeks kept taking sidelong uneasy glances at Ms. Scott. "It's my—" he said, and clutched the edge of the counter with both hands. He licked his lips. He froze at the brink, then plunged: "—my bed."

"Your bed, sir?"

The man leaned forward, and lowered his voice. "It won't stop," he said.

I looked at the desk clerk, to see if this sentence had made any sense to *him*, and was relieved to see it hadn't. Looking baffled, but willing to be of any assistance, the desk clerk said, "It won't stop, sir?"

"No." And here he leaned even further forward, put his left elbow on the counter, and shielded the left side of his face from Ms. Scott with his hand. He was expressing acute sexual embarrassment, such as I remembered from my own experiences at the age of seventeen, when buying condoms; at a drugstore away from my own neighborhood, of course. And frequently for only theoretical use.

The desk clerk now asked the question that I too was dying to hear answered: "It won't stop *what*, sir?"

The man muttered something, at the same time putting his non-shielding hand over his mouth.

The desk clerk leaned forward, with his Polly-want-a-cracker alert look: "Sir?"

"*Vibrating.*" The whisper this time was one of those incredibly loud hard windy sounds; you could have heard it in the parking lot. Immediately, the man shrunk deeper inside his Fu Manchu robe, with a despairing look at the countertop. He wanted to die.

"Oh!" the desk clerk said. "*Vi*-brating!" Everything was clear to him now, except the man's embarrassment.

Well, nothing at all was clear to me. I leaned sideways to look past the man's dragon-populated back toward Ms. Scott, to see if she felt the same bewilderment I did, but I couldn't catch her eye. Having obviously understood the nature of the man's embarrassment, she was trying to ease matters for him by being totally absorbed in a tourist brochure from a resort hotel on Lake Erie. (I myself glanced at this brochure a bit later, and it did have its fascinations. Since Lake Erie water can eat through a human body in under three minutes, a wood or aluminum boat in ten and a steel hull in twenty-five, this resort couldn't offer much by way of the usual swimming and boating. The brochure featured lots of color photographs of people playing croquet.)

But now the desk clerk himself came to the assistance of my understanding, saying to the unhappy man, "You put a quarter in the slot, did you?"

This suggestive phrase almost did for the man completely. Broken, willing to confess to anything if only he could then be given an early quiet execution, he nodded and mumbled, "Yes."

"The bed should vibrate for ten minutes, sir," the desk clerk said. "Soothing you to sleep."

The man himself was in a kind of motion: not so much vibrating as quivering. "It did," he said. "But then it wouldn't stop." In telling his story, he was finding new strength, the will after all to go on. "It woke me up," he explained. "It wouldn't stop. I did everything. I even pushed the 'Coin Return' button. It simply wouldn't stop. It's up there right now," he said, with a gesture upwards of chin and eyebrows, "vibrating."

I couldn't help it; I looked ceilingward. Somewhere in this building, a ravenous insatiable bed was vibrating, all by itself.

"I'm very sorry, sir," the desk clerk said, being brisk and standard now that he understood the situation. He was more a computer than a man, anyway; every possible encounter would be met by a pre-programmed response. (That's why Ms. Scott and I had thrown him off. There was no program for a couple like us.) A vibrating bed obviously called for the broken-TV response: "I'll phone the engineer right now, sir. Could you tell me your room number?"

"Two-fifteen."

The desk clerk repeated the number, in a not entirely convincing show of competence, and turned away to make his call.

Leaving the man to his own devices, between Ms. Scott and me. He flashed her one agonized look—she was still absorbed in photographs of women in long white dresses standing over croquet mallets—then turned his back toward her, hunching his shoulder for added protection; which brought him face to face with me. "I don't like to complain," he told me.

"No, of course not," I said.

"Normally," he said, "I don't even go to bed this early."

"Ah," I said. Eight o'clock *was* early; he had a point there.

"But I have a meeting tomorrow at Wilkes-Barre." Talking seemed to calm him a bit, so he did more of it: "I must be at the airport by four A.M., and I *must* be alert for the meeting. It's *vitally* important."

"Ah," I said.

"Normally, Mr. Wilcox would have handled it," he explained, "but of course Mr. Wilcox is recuperating from his hemorrhoid operation and he, uh—his operation, he's, um, he's recuperating, he, um, his operation—"

The man's very ears were stretching, like Spock on *Star Trek*: had the woman behind him heard the dread word 'hemorrhoid'? Surely if such horrible sexual embarrassment were a genetic trait, in the very nature of the affliction it would have been bred out of the race by now; so it must be a cultural acquisition.

And the man was stuck in it, well and truly stuck, very much like his vibrating bed. Without help, he wasn't *ever* going to struggle past Mr. Wilcox's operation. So I provided help, saying, "Tomorrow's your big chance, is that it?"

"—recuper—Yes!" His gratitude was immense. "That's right!" he cried. "Tomorrow may be the most important day of my career. I *must* be alert and well-rested. I realize it may sound, well, it may sound, um, *odd*, for a grown person to go to bed this early, and to use that, um, that, in the bed. You know, the bed."

"The vibrator."

The poor man turned as red as his robe. "Oh, my God," he whispered. "Is that what they call it?"

"I really don't know. I was guessing." Then, because 'vibrator' was even more paralyzing than 'hemorrhoid,' I helped him again: "But you just wanted to be sure you got your proper sleep," I suggested, "even though it was so early." (I was hoping the word 'proper' would soothe him.)

It did: "That's right! That's exactly it! I may have gone to, um, bed before eight o'clock in the evening, I may have been using that, uh, uh, uh—"

"Machine."

"Machine. Yes. But I do assure you—I assure anyone at all, in fact—" (with slightly raised voice for the benefit of the lady learning all about Lake Erie) "—that my reasons for being there, at that time, and using that, that machine, were strictly business."

"I don't doubt it for a second," I promised him, and at that point the desk clerk returned to the conversation with his own promises, saying, "Sir, the engineer is on his way to your room right now."

"Thank you very much," the man said. "I really don't like to complain."

"Not at all, sir." But then the desk clerk smiled and said, "It's probably just a loose screw."

Unfortunate. The man had been getting calmer and calmer, but that last phrase sent him right up the wall again. "Yes yes yes," he said, backing away from us all, nodding spastically and smiling like a poison victim. "I'm sorry I had to come," he said, then twitched all over like a marionette. Now he was appalling himself. "But I have to snatch what sleep I can," he told us. There was no way out for the poor man; every word he spoke was another electrocution. "It's hard on me!" he wailed, clapped both hands over his mouth, and fled.

# 6

The trouble is, there hadn't been any sexual problem between Ms. Scott and me. You very early learn in this business that a cabdriver is not a man; at least, not to a good-looking woman. Women who wouldn't dream of having a casual chat with a strange man on the sidewalk or in Bloomingdale's will have long relaxed talks with cabdrivers, because they know there's *no possibility of misunderstanding*. And the cabby knows it, too. (The exceptions don't last long.) Women in my cab have told me about their love lives, their operations, their troubles with their mothers, their difficulty with the next-door peeping tom and I don't know what all; if the same women had said the same things at a party, I would have assumed we were in the opening skirmishes of a flirtation. But not in a cab; that's neutral territory, and everybody knows it. It's like a cop not drinking on duty, or a clerk not taking personal calls at the office. You don't even think about it.

But then the man with the unstoppable bed entered our lives, and all at once that morgue-cold Holiday Inn lobby was absolutely tropical with sex. Somewhere in my mind that rampant bed vibrated, while on it, sweat-gleaming and softly butting, writhed—well, all bodies are anonymous once you get to bed, but one of those bodies was very similar in shape to Ms. Scott, standing here beside me at the Holiday Inn counter, demurely filling out her registration form.

Ms. Scott wore no bra, which was nothing out of the ordinary. Many women in New York go braless in summer, and have for several years; the sight of nipple-bump through cloth has long since ceased to astound. I'd been aware of Ms. Scott's breasts from the time she first got into the cab, and—no, from before, when she heaved her two suitcases into the cab ahead of herself. I'd been fully aware then of her breasts, her legs, the slender curve of her hip, the excellent good features of her face—I mean, I'm not blind. But nor am I a crazed billygoat; seeing one attractive and fully clothed woman on the street in the sunshine doesn't exactly make me paw the ground.

So it was a surprise to feel this sudden rising heat. What had happened, that goddam man with his goddam vibrating bed and his goddam sexual nervousness had thrust the *idea* of sex between Ms. Scott and me, and all at once the sexual content of the moment overcame everything else. We were traveling together, unknown by the people around us. We were in a motel together. Somewhere a bed vibrated, and the world filled with men and women having sex together, murmuring and moaning, thrusting and grasping, rolling and tumbling. A great insistent pulsebeat occupied all of life, with Ms. Scott and me at the hot throbbing humid center of it. All at once, I was not the easygoing cabby anymore, I was—I don't know what I was, but it made my hands shake as I tried to write the cab's license plate number on the registration form.

And when I pushed forward my completed registration card, coincidentally at the same moment as Ms. Scott's, so that the edges of our hands accidentally touched, and she started like a fawn, yanking her hand away and staring straight ahead, lips slightly parted, an added touch of color in her cheek, I suddenly realized that *she* was feeling it, too.

But it was only our bodies. Our minds and emotions were engaged only at levels of embarrassment and cover-up. Arousal is only to the point when the mind and emotions agree with the body, which in this case they did not. So we stood there side by side at the counter, dewy, spongy, pliant (her) and priapic (me), and pretended there was nothing going on, while the desk clerk endlessly did things with registration forms and Ms. Scott's credit card and a pair of keys. At last he gave me directions where to drive and park the cab, and Ms. Scott and I thanked him and turned away and went outside.

By then the first heat had faded, we were both dealing in a civilized way with the problem, and she even risked a quick sidelong glance at me as I held the cab door for her. What she saw must have been to some extent reassuring; a faint smile touched her lips as she said, "Thank you."

We were almost conspirators; almost, but not quite. Neither of us could acknowledge to the other what was going on. I got behind the wheel, drove around to the side of the building, parked where the desk clerk had said, and carried my bag and one of Ms. Scott's as we both went up the outside stairs, into the building, and down the long tubular hall to our rooms, which were opposite one another.

Uncertain just how reassured she'd become, I didn't offer to carry her bag inside, and she did seem relieved when I put it down in the doorway. "See you later," I said.

"Thank you," she said again, but when I saw that this time her smile was nervous I stopped hanging around the hall, unlocked my way into my room, threw my bag on the bed—it wasn't vibrating—stripped off my clothing, and took a long cold shower.

## 7

It was just after nine o'clock, the air-conditioner was on full blast, and I lay naked on the bed watching television commercials and thinking vaguely of food, when the phone rang. I frowned at it, irrationally suspecting a practical joke. Who knew me around here?

Ms. Scott, of course. Her calm voice said, "I'm going down to dinner now. I don't promise I'll talk much, but shall we share a table?"

"Give me two minutes."

"Just knock on my door."

Which I did, approximately two minutes later. She had changed to a thin cotton sleeveless dress, with a pale shawl over her bare shoulders; for the air-conditioning, I suppose. I myself had switched from my usual work costume of sneakers, dungarees and a T-shirt to black loafers, gray slacks, and a short-sleeve blue patterned shirt. At least we'd look appropriate at the same table.

The sexual frenzy was out of us now. We could meet one another's eye, we could smile without fear of misinterpretation, and I even automatically took her elbow for a few seconds as we went through a doorway. She was silent on the way downstairs, as she'd promised, but amiable company; as in the cab.

The restaurant was a vast low-ceilinged cavern swathed in patterned drapery and drenched in Muzak. It was hard to believe we weren't ninety feet or more below the surface of the earth, but if we'd actually struggled our way through the drapes to one of the side windows we would have been looking out at ground level toward the main parking lot.

Of the several hundred tables here, perhaps four were occupied, all in the same distant corner of the room. The headwaiter, a thin short pencil-moustached smiler, a kind of pocket Errol Flynn, tried to cram us in among the rest of his customers, but Ms. Scott—bless her—pointed to a table a sensible distance away and said, "Why not that one?"

Why not, indeed? We were spoiling some mathematically precise plan inside his head, that's why not, but there was nothing he could do about it short of drawing a pistol and forcing us to sit where he wanted. With very bad grace, he led us to the table Ms. Scott had indicated, and left us there alone for a long time. I detected a few of the other diners looking enviously in our direction, obviously wishing they too had had the courage to tell our friend they didn't feel like eating *en campement* tonight; while we waited for the headwaiter to get over his sulk and bring menus, I commented to Ms. Scott: "Too many people allow themselves to get pushed around in restaurants."

She smiled in agreement, but said, "I hope you didn't mind my taking charge that way."

"You're in charge," I pointed out. "If I was taking you out, I'd have picked that table over there."

She frowned over at the table I'd randomly chosen, wondering why it was better than this one; then looked back at me, frowned a second longer, and suddenly smiled, saying, "I see. Thank you."

"You have enough to think about," I told her, "without also having to worry if my male ego is being trampled on. It isn't."

"I didn't think it was, but thanks for the reassurance."

"Can we laugh now about the man with the unstoppable bed?"

She did laugh, but she said, "Maybe," and at the same time gestured very strongly at the headwaiter, whose unwary eye she had caught with a look of steel.

He came over, then, and said to me, "Sir?"

"I didn't call you," I said.

"We'd like menus," Ms. Scott told him. "And I think drinks. Yes?" That last to me.

"Gin and tonic would be nice," I acknowledged.

"And vodka and tonic for me." Ms. Scott smiled coolly at the headwaiter and then, as though he'd already left, said to me, "How many miles did we do today?"

Beneath the headwaiter's pencil moustache, as he departed, were pursed lips. I said, "Just under six hundred."

"Isn't that a lot, in one day?"

"It's different from Sixth Avenue," I admitted. "To tell the truth, at first I was enjoying myself, but toward the end I wouldn't have minded doing something else."

"Ten hours a day is too much," she said. "From now on, just do what's comfortable, and stop when you're tired."

I wasn't sure myself if I wanted to keep on at the same pace. "Thanks for giving me the option."

"Of course. Um— May I call you Thomas?"

"I wish you wouldn't," I said. "Nobody else does. Try Tom."

"Tom. Fine. And I'm Katharine."

"Not Kathy or Kate?"

"No," she said, as though people who called her those names were never heard from again.

I persisted: "Not Kit or Kitty or Kat?"

Finally she laughed. "Now, look, Thomas," she said.

"Katharine," I said.

"And Tom." She extended a slim hand across the table. "How do you do?"

"Fine, thanks," I said, taking her hand. "And you?"

"Very well."

The handshake ended as the drinks arrived, brought by a

pleasant overweight high school girl who also left us menus the size of garage doors. I counted how often the word "succulent" was used in the menus (8), and when the girl came back I ordered the creamed herring, the Junior Sirloin (I think you're supposed to feel less than a man if you don't order the King), the baked potato, no vegetable, and the mixed green salad. Looking at me, she said, "And wine?"

"Certainly."

There was a tiny folded wine list that lived on the table amid the condiments. Katharine consulted it briefly and said, "The Almaden Pinot Noir."

The waitress, who'd been efficiently and cheerfully writing everything in her pad, now stumbled to a halt. "The what?"

Katharine said it again, then a third time, then finally pointed to it on the wine list. "Oh!" said the girl, copied it down laboriously from the list, and went away.

I said, "How do you suppose *she* pronounces it?"

"I doubt she ever has." Then she gave me a keen look, and said, "Do you mind if I ask a snobbish question?"

Putting on my awful imitation Brooklyn accent, I said, "Yuh mean, why deny tawk like uh cabdrivuh?"

Her smile was apologetic. "I'm afraid so, yes."

"Then I'll tell you my story." I sipped gin and tonic, and began: "I am downwardly mobile. My father pushed a hack around New York for twenty-five years so I'd have the advantages he didn't have. I went to college, I learned to wear ties and suits, I came out and married a tall girl and became an executive trainee with Retrieval Data Corporation. Ever hear of them?"

"No."

"I was a junior executive there for five years. I hated it. Also I went on being married, and I lived in New Brunswick, New

Jersey. Do you know just how horrible New Brunswick, New Jersey is?"

She smiled faintly, as she shook her head. "No, I don't."

"You're lucky. Those who do have experience of New Brunswick, New Jersey are scarred for life. Anyway, Retrieval Data went under three years ago, one of the several thousand computer companies that couldn't survive the recession. That was just around the time my wife left me, so I—"

"Do you have children?"

I shook my head. "I didn't want any and she couldn't have any. The lack of family was one of our strongest bonds. She left me for a widower with four daughters."

"Oh," she said.

"So I came back to New York," I finished, "and got a temporary job for the rest of my life driving my father's cab days. He won't let me have it nights. And I'm happy as a clam."

"How about your father?"

"He would like to be a junior executive. Failing that, he would like *me* to be a junior executive. Failing *that*, he would like me not to rack up the cab."

She was looking concerned for me: "But what's going to happen to you now?"

"It's happening. Except for this. Going to California, this is something different, kind of an adventure."

"But are you really just going to drive a cab the rest of your life?"

"Why not? It's socially utile, it keeps me in contact with the general public, it affords me a constantly changing milieu, it pays the rent and it's fun."

The girl came then with the artichoke and the herring, and we paused in our conversation to eat. The herring was standard fare, but the artichoke was just the heart, chopped up and floating in vinegar and oil. Katharine didn't seem charmed by it, but she ate it without comment, and as she was finishing the headwaiter showed up, lugging a chinkling ice bucket on a stand. Placing it beside our table, he took from it an unopened bottle of wine and showed me the label.

Jesus, he was a slow learner. "The lady ordered it," I said.

He had been hoping to have no further dealings with the lady for the rest of his life. With wrinkled mouth and wrinkled moustache he reluctantly turned one hundred eighty degrees, presenting the bottle.

Meantime, Katharine had been frowning at the ice bucket with understandable perplexity, and now she said, "But this is red wine."

"Isn't this what you ordered?" He showed her the label.

"Yes, yes." She gave the label an impatient look and nod. "That's what I ordered, but you don't *chill* red wine."

He had never known anyone who was so much trouble. "*All* our wines are chilled," he said, with condescending pride. "It's the way it's done."

"Well—" I could see her contemplating the conversation that would ensue if she even *started* to explain things, and I could also see her wisely decide to cut the Gordian knot. She said, "Do you have any wine that *hasn't* been chilled?"

"All of our wine is on ice." So was his manner.

She looked over at me. "Shall we take it anyway?"

I liked that; she was making it a question between equals. I shrugged and said, "We'll warm it in our palms, like brandy."

"All right," she said, and told the headwaiter, "you might as well open it."

He did so, looking miffed and making less of a production than he might have done, then poured each of our glasses half full without waiting for one of us to taste the wine and accept it, and placed the dripping bottle in the middle of the table, saying, "You won't be wanting the cooler?"

Katharine said, "The what? Oh, the ice bucket. No, thank you."

With frozen dignity he picked up the 'cooler' and chinkle-binked away with it. I tasted the wine, which was very cold indeed, and therefore thin and watery. "Well, it isn't sour," I said.

"No, but our friend is."

Then the girl came with our main courses, which were perfectly fine; except of course that the baked potato wasn't really a baked potato. It was a steamed potato, inside the aluminum foil. Oh, well; you take the rough with the smooth. By the time we'd finished eating, the wine had warmed considerably, and wasn't at all bad.

Neither of us wanted coffee or dessert. Katharine ordered the bill, the headwaiter handed it to me, and I handed it back. Neither Katharine nor I said anything, so he put it in the dead center of the table, leaning against the sugar, and departed.

As Katharine studied the bill, I said, "This could get annoying, all the way across the country."

"I'm used to it," she said. "I frequently have business lunches with men, where I'm paying. Waiters just can't adapt to the idea."

"Sure they can. They don't want to."

"A political statement?" She seemed to consider the idea for the first time. "You may be right."

"Down with the liberated woman."

With a thin smile she said, "It saves me quite a bit on tips." Then she signed the bill, with her room number, and added the gratuity; I didn't see how much, but the writing was small.

We went back upstairs and parted at our rooms, agreeing to

meet for breakfast at eight. I phoned the desk and left a seven-thirty call, then kicked off my shoes, switched on the TV, and sprawled on the bed. It wasn't yet ten-thirty. I lay there watching the colors and thinking about Katharine Scott. Nice lady. Difficult for women to move around in the world, with everybody trying to shove them down behind the nearest man. A lot of men would not have been able to resist the impulse to 'help' her tonight, with the desk clerk or the headwaiter; especially the headwaiter. Fortunately, I'm quiescent by nature.

I wondered about Barry, the man in her life, toward whom we were making haste slowly. Would he have 'handled' things this evening? Probably. Soon it would be his job anyway; I presumed Katharine would be over her skittishness by the time we reached Los Angeles, and would then marry him and settle down. She'd go on being a landscape architect, of course, and go on having trouble with waiters at business lunches, but the rest of the time Barry would be in charge. Women are like bewitched characters in old legends, sometimes capable of coping with ordinary life and motion, and at other times under a spell that makes it impossible for them to open doors or order a meal. But instead of the prince's kiss breaking the spell, it finishes the job of locking the spell on for life.

I thought Barry probably wasn't good enough for her. On the other hand, neither was I.

# 8

At breakfast, Katharine suddenly broke a silence by saying, "Whatever happened to the girl in the cab?"

*Katharine* was the girl in the cab; wasn't she? I said, "What?"

"The one who wanted to commit suicide, but she was afraid of heights. That was a true story, wasn't it?"

"Of course," I said. "All my stories are true. She was going to jump out of the cab when it reached sixty."

"But the air pressure is too strong on the doors at that speed."

"That's right."

"Whatever happened to her, do you know?"

"She married the cabby."

"Oh," she said.

## 9

We were on the road by nine-thirty, and had soon crossed the border into Indiana. It was a clear sunny day, with the kind of crisp air in which other cars' chrome winks at you from half a mile off. The countryside was green and rolling farmland, with neither Pennsylvania's tumbled mountains nor Ohio's industrial slag. Clusters of red barns and herds of grazing cows in the long green folds were sunlit illustrations from a children's book, serene and timeless. The cab rolled like a yellow marble through the landscape that seemed never to have known war, or want, or even winter.

Katharine was less tense this morning, did less brooding and more sightseeing, but remained silent. As for me, I stayed up front with my steering wheel and my thoughts, such as they were—mostly I thought about how nice it would be to have a radio. The two-way radio in the cab wasn't the sort to pick up local AM or FM stations.

We reached Indianapolis around eleven-thirty, and picked our way through the tangle of bypass roads. Yesterday we'd done the same with Akron and Columbus, so now I noticed for the third time how the local traffic in and near the cities contains a much higher percentage of old and beat-up cars. And pick-up trucks; you get on a major highway through a large city, you're going to see an awful lot of grungy pick-up trucks.

Indianapolis was the first place where I really began to attract the attention of the drivers around me. No, let me rephrase that: Indianapolis was the first place where the drivers around me began deliberately to attract *my* attention. Cars would pull up beside me and honk, and when I'd look over there the driver would be, expressing all kind of humorous astonishment: What on *Earth* is a New York City taxicab doing in *Indianapolis*? he would ask, by means of eyebrows, hand gestures, big grins, mouthed words, head shakings, and other expressions of bafflement. Beats me, I would answer, by grinning and shrugging and shaking my head. If the guy persisted—I mean, how was I to answer the question car-to-car at 60 miles an hour even if I wanted to?—I just kept shrugging, waved a friendly bye-bye, and gradually slackened speed until he gave up.

The major cities cut your time, even with the Interstates. Mostly you can do 70 or 80 through the countryside—except for those few states that take the 55-mile-an-hour limit seriously—but the traffic build-up in the cities slows you to 60 or even less. We were nearly half an hour circling Indianapolis, and as we were leaving the city behind—without actually having seen it at all—Katharine moved forward to the jump seat and said, "Is it all right if we talk for a while?"

"Sure. What's on your mind?"

"Marriage," she said. I laughed, but she only grinned, and then she said, "Would you tell me about *your* marriage?"

"We had a wedding," I said, "and then we had a divorce."

"How much time in between?"

"Five years."

Her forearms were spread across the top of the seat, right hand over left, chin resting on the back of her right hand. From what I could see of her face in the mirror, she was looking concerned for me. She said, "Is it painful to talk about?"

"No, it's just I don't have anything new to say. Everything everybody has ever said about marriage is true, and I don't have anything to add."

"Did you like being married?"

"*Like* it? You don't *like* marriage, you love it and you hate it." I moved my head to get her image clearly in the mirror. "You've never been married?"

"No," she said.

"I hate to do oneupmanship," I said, "but I think this really is one of those cases where you have to have been there."

"Maybe if you just talked about your marriage," she said, "just anything at all that occurs to you, it might start making sense to me."

"Okay," I said, and shifted to a more comfortable position. "Let's see—I was twenty-two when we got married, and she was twenty. Her name was Lynn—well, it still is, isn't it? That part doesn't change. What's Barry's last name?"

"Gilbert."

"Katharine Gilbert," I said it slowly, savoring the syllables. "That's not bad."

"I've written it a thousand times," she told me, "and it's always looked perfectly fine. On the other hand, I'm so used to being Katharine Scott—" She sat up straighter, shaking her head. "I've been it all my life." Then she shrugged, still looking dubious, and said, "I suppose you adjust."

"You could do that hyphen thing," I suggested. "Katharine Scott-Gilbert."

"But what if I had a daughter? Say I named her—I don't know—Jane. So she'd grow up Jane Scott-Gilbert, and then she marries a man named Jones, and *she* hyphenates, and she winds up Jane Scott-Gilbert-Jones."

"Actually, it's your granddaughter I feel sorry for," I said. "Anita Scott-Gilbert-Jones-Marmaduke."

She reared back to stare at me. "Marmaduke?"

"They make the best husbands."

She grinned, then leaned forward to rest her chin on her hands again, saying, "And what sort of husband did *you* make?"

Persistent woman. "C minus," I told her.

"What did you do wrong?"

"I adapted badly. Or maybe I grew up crooked, I'm still not sure."

"Tell me about— What was it, Lynn?"

"Lynn Rushton Fletcher."

"Did *she* hyphenate?"

"No," I said. "But that could be another problem with the hyphen: divorce and marriage. By now, Lynn could be Lynn Rushton-Fletcher-Heffernan. And that's with only one false start."

"On that basis," Katharine said, "I know women who'd take five minutes just to tell you who they were."

"There aren't enough hyphens in the whole world."

"The great hyphen shortage."

"That's right," I said. "Price going up, stock market going down."

"If it doesn't bother you to talk about your marriage," she said, "why do you keep changing the subject?"

"Do I? I have a short attention span, that was one of our problems. How would *you* like it if the guy you're married to wakes up every morning, looks at you, frowns, and then snaps his fingers and says, 'Oh, yeah, I remember!'?"

She gave me a skeptical look and said, "Do you remember my question?"

"Okay, officer," I said. "I'll come quietly."

"Tell me about Lynn."

"I met her in college. She was a photography major. After I graduated and got the job with RDC, Lynn quit school in her third year and we got married."

"Did she get a job?"

"No, she went on with the photography. She specialized in animal pictures; mostly horses and dogs. Domestic animals, not wild."

"Was she good at it?"

"As a matter of fact, yes. She sold a lot of pictures. Calendars, greeting cards, a couple of magazine features. She even got some portrait commissions, people who had pedigree dogs or racehorses or whatever."

"So it wasn't just a hobby."

"Not a bit of it. She bought a Ford Econoline van, strictly out of her own money, and fixed up the back as a combination bedroom-darkroom. Weekends, we used to drive all over the northeast; dog shows, horse shows, racetracks, things like that."

"Sounds like fun."

"It was, sort of. But I never got used to those darkroom smells, the van was full of them. We'd sleep in back on a Friday or Saturday night, and I'd have the weirdest dreams of my life, all from the chemical smells."

"Were you taking pictures, too?"

"Not me. I don't have a head for photography. You hand me an Instamatic and I stand directly in front of something and go snap, and the picture is this simple dull factual statement. 'Flower,' it says, or 'Two people on a front lawn.' With complicated cameras I don't actually take any pictures at all. I get bogged down with the light meter or the lens opening, and gradually disappear in the quicksand of technology."

"Did Lynn try to teach you?"

"She offered, a couple times."

The questions stopped, then, and when I looked in the mirror she was ruminating at my profile, thinking over what she'd learned so far.

I could have told her not to waste the energy. I too used to ponder my marriage, both during and after, and it never made any sense to me, so how could it make sense to anybody else? It was like Katharine telling me that Barry was a plastic surgeon, and then showing me his pictures—two completely different impressions, both of them probably a little bit right and a lot wrong.

I'd described Lynn to people before, and hearing myself I knew I always made her sound like one of those healthy hearty big-assed women whose motto is Can-Do and whose flaw is they can't actually *see* any other human beings. I myself know—or to some extent I think I know—how much that image approaches the truth of who Lynn is, but there are so many other elements left out that in fact the impression I'm giving is completely false. And the reason I long ago gave up trying to correct that false impression is there's no way to do it.

If I had a photo of Lynn I could show it now, and Katharine would see the snub nose and the very curly short black hair and the large sympathetic eyes, and then she could put *that* face behind the camera taking the picture of the best-of-breed Weimaraner on his dog-show pedestal, and to that extent Lynn would become a bit more human in Katharine's mind, as Barry had become in mine. But could I describe, to take just one example, Lynn's relationship with orange juice? That absorbed meticulousness when extracting the frozen concentrate from the can, adding precisely three cans of cold water, stirring, frowning, leaning close to the Lucite jug to peer into the orange depths for still-frozen lumps, the total absorption of the ultimate alchemist making orange gold from frozen lead, culminating in that beautiful sunny smile as in comic triumph she carries the two gleaming orange glasses out ahead of herself to the breakfast table, so that any day that started with the opening of a new orange juice can would be sunny and happy for both of us all the way through—could I describe that repeated morning scene, against all kinds of weather through the kitchen window beyond her rapt head, and my own feelings of tenderness entangled in it? And if I did manage to get some flavor of that moment across, even to the extent that it altered a bit further Katharine's image of Lynn, what would be the point? She would still be far far far from the truth—even so much of the truth as I happen to know.

In fact, it's impossible to describe a person to another person; the best you can do is a caricature approximation. Only lovers ever try for more than that, and while I still did love Lynn—you must either love or hate an ex-wife; indifference is not possible—it was not an active or combustible love. It was more like the love between brother and sister who used to fight a lot and who now live in different cities and rarely communicate. All of which means that Katharine was now trying to plumb the depths of a marriage between a cabby she'd just met and an inaccurate caricature in her own mind. Good luck.

While she went on pushing that particular boulder uphill, I concentrated on my driving. Traffic had eased again to a trickle, now that we'd left Indianapolis well behind, and I was traveling between 75 and 80, using my outside mirrors to reassure myself no Smokies were clocking me. Then, after about ten minutes of silence, Katharine spoke again:

"What did you do on those weekends while your wife was taking pictures?"

So she knew she needed more information. "A lot of reading," I told her.

"You're not interested in animals?"

"If I see a cat or a dog on the street I say hello. That's about as far as it goes."

"You didn't have pets when you were a boy?"

"We lived in an apartment in Queens. Also, more important, my mother believes animals carry germs that kill people on contact."

"Did you miss having pets?"

"You can't miss what you've never had," I said. "Also, friends of mine had pets, and nothing in those relationships ever made me envious. Also I was an only child, which meant *I* was a pet."

She gave me a keen look, as though I'd just revealed a very important fact. But that's okay; people always give you a keen look when you say you're an only child. There's general agreement that it's a very important clue, like bedwetting, but I don't think anybody's sure what the clue *means*. It's just a clue, like the footprint outside the library window.

Katharine absorbed this clue for a minute or so, then went back to her general line of questioning. "So your whole part in these weekends," she said, "was just the van. Driving it and fixing it up."

"Just driving it. Lynn fixed it up, it was her baby."

"*Her* baby or her *baby*?"

I sighed. "Well," I said, "the evil that *Freud* did certainly lives after him."

She had the grace to look embarrassed, saying, "You're right. Sorry."

But I wanted to make sure she understood. "Lynn lives now with five kids—they adopted one—plus dogs, plus cats, and she's still an animal photographer. Last time I saw her she'd switched from the van up to a big Winnebago, fixed it up inside all by herself. With the kids' help."

"So the point is," Katharine said, "they aren't just substitutes."

"That's right. She was really interested in photography *and* animals *and* the van."

"And you were strictly the chauffeur."

"You can take the cabby out of the cab, but…" I shrugged. "As I keep trying to explain to my father."

"Oh, that's right, your father," she said. "That was the same time you had the job you didn't like. During the week you tried to please your father, and on weekends you tried to please your wife. That doesn't leave much for *you*."

"Well, I didn't need much. I'm not saying I was downtrodden or anything. My father and Lynn both have definite ideas about life, that's all. If I had definite ideas I'd make a fuss about them, the way they do. But I don't, so I just go along."

"Up to a point. You are driving this cab."

"Temporarily."

"Temporarily for the rest of your life. That's what you said."

"Well, anyway, it's only because RDC folded. If it hadn't I'd still be there."

"What about the marriage?"

"She left me. She said we didn't have an actual marriage, we had a teenage romance that we were the wrong age for. She said I wasn't serious. As a matter of fact, I'm not serious. I mean, if we suddenly had a blowout here in the cab, left front tire, I'd be *very* serious, I'd struggle with the wheel and bring us to a safe stop and all, I wouldn't be a Harpo Marx at the controls here, but as long as things are going smoothly I'm not a serious person at all."

All of which she was finding very distressing. "But sooner or later," she said, "you *have* to be serious."

"Why?"

"Your wife was right, you have to grow up, you can't be a thirty-year-old man with a temporary job."

"A lot of thirty-year-old men have temporary jobs. The difference is, I know it."

She was getting annoyed with me. "Well, if you're just going to say that nothing matters…"

I stood my ground; or sat my cab. "As a matter of fact," I said, "most things *don't* matter. Never put off till tomorrow what you can put off till next week is the best approach to life I know of."

"But that's what *I've* been doing," she said, "for the last two years, and if there's one thing I know, it's that I've been immature. It's very immature to avoid grown-up decisions."

"Indecision is the key to flexibility."

She stared at me. "What?"

"Indecision," I repeated, "is the key to flexibility."

"But what does that *mean*?"

"Take your problem with Barry," I said. "You have to decide between 'yes' and 'no,' and the assumption is there's a right answer. So the *other* assumption is, there's a wrong answer. You don't know which is which, so for two years you haven't made any decision at all, and the result is, for two years you haven't made a mistake."

"Oh, come on. Now you're making a virtue of copping out."

"Of course I am. Two years of not making a mistake—that's a pretty good record for a human being."

"Well, now I *have* to decide. I can't stall any longer."

"Unfortunately," I agreed, "there are the moments like that. A part of the game plan for a successful life is to try to avoid as many of those moments as possible. For instance, that's why this job is only temporary. If I decided it was permanent I'd have a fight with my father. Also, to be perfectly honest, with myself, because I'm not sure I *want* to drive a cab the rest of my life. I might want to be a fireman instead, or run for Congress, or be an insurance company claims examiner. I'm indecisive."

She laughed, losing her irritation with me. That was one of

her best qualities; she could always be jollied out of too much seriousness. But, having laughed, she nevertheless said, "Well, I *can't* be indecisive. Not anymore."

"You're doing your best, though," I pointed out. "You got an extra five, six days just by taking this cab instead of the plane."

"That's right." She surprised me by seeming surprised. "That's why I'm doing this, isn't it? Still stalling."

"You hadn't noticed?"

"But when we get to Los Angeles," she said firmly, "*then* it's final. I *can't* stall anymore, and I *won't* stall anymore. You make immaturity sound very good, Tom, you argue the case beautifully, but the fact is, if you're going to get anywhere in life you have to make decisions."

"Where do you want to get, in life?"

She wouldn't rise to the bait. "To Los Angeles," she said.

"Okay, lady," I said. "You're the customer."

Lunch from a McDonald's near Terre Haute, then across another state line and our first new time zone: Illinois; Central Time. Katharine had returned to her brooding after our long talk, and following lunch she brought out the pencil and legal pad and did a lot of writing. As for me, I wondered if my glib praise of juvenility had had any effect on her. I hoped not; I'd only talked that way to pass the time. Not that I disagreed with myself; passivity was certainly the best game plan I'd ever found for my own situation. On the other hand, I knew it was wrong for most people, and at the moment useless for Katharine Scott. She *had* to make a decision, whether she wanted to or not. Her real difficulty wasn't in solving the problem but in facing it, and she'd have to know that before she could break through.

I was pondering this magazine-psychology-article wisdom when I noticed, some distance ahead, a car parked at the side of the road, and a fellow actually standing *in* the road, running back and forth from lane to lane and urgently waving his arms crosswise above his head. Tapping my brakes, I said over my shoulder, "Something."

Katharine peered past me at the road. "What is it?"

"Beats me."

As I pulled off on the shoulder and came to a stop behind the other car, I saw that steam was pouring from its radiator and that it contained at least one passenger. Meanwhile, the man came hurrying over to my window and cried, "You have to take us to town!"

"Sorry, Mac," I said. "I've already got a fare."

"It's my wife!"

Was that a woman in the other car? I said, "If you want, I'll stop at the next gas station, have them come—"

"No time! No time! We have to get to the hospital!"

"Hospital?" And then I knew, and I thought, *Oh, no.*

"My wife!" he cried, and said the dreadful words: "She's about to have a baby!"

"Oh, for God's sake," I said.

Katharine said, "A baby?"

"We were rushing to the hospital, the car broke down, I've got to—" And he broke off to yell at the car, "Myra! Come on, darling!"

Before I could say anything, before I could figure out some semi-decent way out of this, Katharine had leaped from the cab and was running over to the other car, where an extremely pregnant woman was now ponderously emerging. Her husband dashed over to help, and he and Katharine walked the woman to the cab and helped her into the back. "Thank God you came by!" the man cried.

"Yeah, yeah," I said.

"Bless you," said the woman. Her forehead was pebble-grained with perspiration. "Bless you for this."

"Sure," I said.

The couple got settled in back, Katharine slid into the front next to me—knocking all my roadmaps on the floor—and off we went, scattering gravel in our wake. I kept the accelerator pressed right down on the floor, and behind me the man yelled, "It's the next exit, about five miles down the road! Then take the left toward town!"

"Right, right."

"We'll make it, darling," he told his wife.

"We damn well better," I muttered.

Beside me, Katharine was all excited and bright-eyed, her head first turning back to look at the woman and then forward to watch the rapidly unreeling highway. "Do you think we *will* make it?" she asked.

"You better hope we do."

"Well, it has happened before," she told me. "The *Daily News* constantly runs stories about women having babies in taxicabs."

"Yeah," I said, "but what the *Daily News* doesn't run is what happens next. You ever been around childbirth?"

"No," she said, looking doubtful. "Why? What's wrong?"

"It's a mess, that's what's wrong. The human body is a wonderful thing, so long as everything that's inside *stays* inside. Once the inside stuff starts coming out, what you've got is a mess. A cabby I know had it happen to him, a woman giving birth in the back of the cab, and not *only* did it cost him an arm and a leg to get the cab cleaned it also took two days to air the thing out before he could use it again. Two days out of business. Romance is romance, but real life is real life, and believe me, Katharine, you do not want to travel to Los Angeles in a cab in which somebody has just given birth."

"Oh," she said.

"I don't want to be mean," I said, because I was afraid that's exactly what I was being, "but if I can possibly avoid it I would rather not get into the Guinness Book of Records as the driver of the New York City cab that was the farthest from New York when a baby was born in it."

That made her laugh. "It would be an interesting record, though," she said. "You have to admit that. Almost worth it."

"Almost," I agreed, and took the exit on two wheels, and turned left. We traveled about a mile on bumpy blacktop country road and then abruptly we reached civilization.

Town turned out to be fairly good-sized, with a lot of slow-moving traffic down the sleepy broad main shopping street. I drove with one hand permanently pressed on the horn, but unfortunately New York City law doesn't permit cabs to have horns loud enough for situations like this one, so instead of going SNARRRLLLL as I swerved and skidded through the slalom of Friday afternoon shoppers, I more or less went *nnnnnnnnnnnnnnnnnn*: more like a bee than an express train. What I needed was a tractor-trailer's big airhorn. "Move! Move! Move!" I screamed at bewildered shoppers as we tore by.

The guy's shouted directions from the back seat were clear and simple: Just keep going. At the far end of the shopping street—in my wake were a lot of open mouths and wide eyes and ashen faces—I should take the street that angles right and up the hill. Check. And that big brick building up at the top is the hospital. And the emergency entrance is around to the left side. And the three people dressed in white *jumped* out of the driveway as I came squealing and whining around the curve, slamming on the brakes at the last possible second and slewing to a stop like a skier, the right edge of the rear bumper just kissing the brick wall beside the entrance.

A white-garbed man who'd been seated on a folding chair beside the door, reading a comic book, was now quivering on his feet with his back pressed to the wall—my right front fender had punted his chair across the driveway as he was leaving it— and I at once leaped from the cab to yell at him across its roof, "Pregnancy! Quick!"

"Right!" He dropped the comic book, spun, and ran through the glass doors into the hospital. The people I hadn't quite hit on the way in were now trotting this way, and I did believe I could hear a siren of some sort coming from town.

Sticking my head in through the open cab window I yelled, "Get her OUT!"

He already was, I'll say that much for him. He couldn't keep his goddam car in good repair, he *and* his wife let things delay until the last possible minute, but I will give him credit for that much: he was getting her out.

Katharine helped. So did the two men who came rushing from the hospital with a wheeled stretcher. They got her out of the cab and onto the stretcher, and damned if that woman didn't start giving birth as they were pushing her through the doorway. I last saw the cluster of them—wife, husband, stretcher, several attendants—all running at top speed down the corridor into the dim interior of the hospital. And bon voyage to them all.

As I turned to watch the two police cars approaching along the driveway, Katharine came over to stand beside me and say, "See? A person can stall and delay too long for their own good. They should have made their decision to come to the hospital this morning."

"The decision those two got wrong was nine months ago," I said, and reached for my wallet. Pretty soon now, I suspected, somebody would be wanting to see my driver's license.

## 11

The interview with the police took place in a small gray-walled office near Emergency. Katharine sat on a green vinyl sofa off to the side while the rest of us stood, except for one cop who half hitched his rump onto a corner of the gray metal desk that was the room's principal piece of furniture.

The officers didn't make an awful lot of trouble, once they understood the situation, though one of them couldn't resist pulling the sort of cheapshot remark so beloved of cops: "Is that the way you drive in New York?"

"Absolutely," I said. "Every time I have a woman giving birth in the back seat."

One of the other cops—five of them were clustered around me—offered a genial smile and said, "Well, we don't want to wipe a lot of other citizens *off* the planet while helping a new one arrive."

This whole situation had made me a little tense, so instead of letting the remarks go I kept answering: "How many did I kill?"

"This time you were lucky."

"Lucky? I thought I was skillful."

"Then the people of the town were lucky," the cop said, with a dry smile. "Lucky you had so much skill."

Another of the cops—the oldest—said, "Well, let's not get excited all over again. Whether it was luck or skill is up to you, but all's well that ends well as far as I'm concerned, and I understand mother and baby are both doing fine."

"Good."

"But," said the cop, "you know what fascinates me."

I did, but he told me anyway.

"What on *Earth* is a New York City taxicab doing in south-central Illinois?"

"Well," I said, "I've got a fare." And I gestured at Katharine, over there on the sofa.

The cops all looked at her, and the one who'd expressed the big question said, in utter bewilderment, "You mean, you two aren't *together*?"

I knew what he meant, of course. "She's my customer," I said.

The cop said, "Miss—" (Cops haven't learned 'Ms' yet.) "Miss," he said, "could I ask where you're going in this taxicab?"

"Los Angeles," she said.

"And where did you get *into* the cab?"

"New York," she said.

I explained, "Had to be New York, I'm not permitted to pick up fares outside the five boroughs. Newark, for instance. I mean the airport, not the city, I wouldn't particularly *want* to pick up fares in the city of Newark, but people coming in to Newark airport are mostly headed for New York. You get runs out there all the time, but you have to travel back empty, and that means—"

"Just a minute," said the cop. "I'm sure that's all very interesting, but what fascinates *me*—" And he told us again.

Well, they must have killed an extra twenty minutes of our valuable time before we'd managed to answer every possible question they could think of to ask. The idea of a woman making haste slowly to her marriage intrigued them at first almost as much as the physical fact of the New York cab in their territory, but they soon sheared away from that aspect. They didn't quite know what to make of Katharine. Was she just a dumbass broad and all she needs is a good screwing from a real man (such as themselves), or was she something else, and if so, what? After a while I noticed a couple of the cops squinting whenever they looked at her, as though she were hard to see— some sort of glare in the way.

Finally it was the discomfort they felt about Katharine that ended the Twenty Questions session. They agreed they wouldn't press charges on all the illegal things I'd done while hurrying through their town—"reckless endangerment" was one of the phrases being bandied about in the early stages—and at last they said we could go. "Drive carefully," one of them told me.

The hell with it; let them have the last word.

On our way out we met an intern who said, "Would you like to see the baby?"

What I'd like to see was the cab and Route 70—this sidetrip was costing us a lot of time—but Katharine at once said, "Would that be possible?"

"Of course. I believe they've just now brought her to the nursery."

"Her? A girl?"

"That's right." He gave us directions—hallways, and then an elevator, and then more hallways—and Katharine thanked him, and we went to look at the baby.

It was one of those viewing windows, like in the movies. Through the glass we could see a fairly large and very clean cream-colored room with lots of chrome machinery against the walls. About half a dozen tiny cribs on wheels were dotted at random around the open floor space, and two starched young nurses were doing this and that. They looked brisk, efficient and incomprehensible. One of them noticed us standing there and came over to open the door beside the viewing window, releasing the sound of screaming baby: it looked so much more peaceful through the soundproof window. She smiled at us, apparently oblivious to the screaming, and said, "What name, please?"

I didn't follow. "*My* name?"

"The family name."

"Oh. Well— Come to think of it, I don't *know* the family name."

She disapproved. "I'm sorry, sir, but family only are permitted to view."

Katharine said, "They told us downstairs we could see the baby."

"They did? Who did?"

"In Emergency," she said. "We're the ones—"

"Oh, the *taxi*! Was it your taxi?"

"It's my father's, actually," I said.

"That's Baby Blodgett," she told us. "I'll bring her right over." And she closed the door—no more baby screams—and went away to choose one of the little cribs and wheel it over by the window. And that was one of the screamers; that head was all mouth and it was wide open.

It wasn't what you could call a beautiful baby, but in my opinion damn few are. This one seemed to be an assemblage made of slightly undercooked bacon; pink and white and wrinkled and rubbery. I looked at it for half a minute or so, then glanced at Katharine and saw her smiling fondly at the squalling hideous creature. I said, "You want one of those?"

She gave me an arch sidelong look: "You volunteering?"

"Not me, lady. I just thought every woman wanted children."

"Because of your ex-wife?"

"Because of what the culture tells me."

"Oh. All right." She studied the bacon puff again for a few seconds, and then said, "Oh, I suppose so. At one time or another, every woman I suppose thinks she'd like to have a baby."

"That's what I understood."

"But even if you have one," she said, "you don't get to keep it."

"Why not?"

"Time," she said, and turned to look at me full face, with a kind of wistful smile. "You start off with a sweet little marsh-mallow like that," she said inaccurately, "and the first thing you know time has gone by and you've got a great big monster lunkhead like you, breaking his father's heart."

"What a pretty baby," I said.

## 12

What with Baby Blodgett, and before that the delay of circling Indianapolis, it was five o'clock before we'd finished crossing Illinois, with St. Louis dead ahead. I had my choices of Interstate bypasses, but at five P.M. it wouldn't really matter what route I took through the city. All arteries, to coin a phrase, would be clogged.

At first, as we neared the city, most of the traffic build-up was outbound, but soon the traffic in both directions got thicker and thicker, until we were barely crawling along amid all the rump-sprung green Impalas and nervous orange Toyotas and the inevitable black pick-up truck with the old refrigerator standing up in back. And the campers, let's not forget all those campers waveringly driven in the wrong gear by the sour old guys in baseball caps with their sour old wives beside them. Slower and slower we went, until even Katharine, who'd been back to brooding herself ever since we'd left the hospital, noticed that something had changed. Coming forward to the jump seat she said, "What's the problem?"

"Rush hour."

"Where are we?"

"St. Louis is off that way," I said, waving a hand to the left.

"Then that bridge must be the Mississippi."

"By golly, you're right." I'd been too involved in the road and the traffic to think about the real world along the way. The Mississippi River; think of that. I'd never crossed it before, not at ground level, and you don't get the same effect in an airplane at thirty-two thousand feet.

Given the traffic situation, we had plenty of time to study the Big Miss as we inched across the bridge, and I must say it was something of a letdown. The Mississippi River had become a major legend in the American mind, like Paul Bunyan or George Washington's cherry tree, with the difference that the river actually exists and can be seen. And it isn't that much to look at, at least not as far north as St. Louis. It's sluggish, and flanked by the usual flotsam of warehouses and barges and decaying river industry, and it isn't even very wide, not in comparison with some other rivers I could mention. It's simply a river, and it can't bear the weight of myth that we've all given it.

I commented on this to Katharine, who assured me other sections of the river did live up to the image, and mentioned a riverside park she'd "done" near Memphis. "You don't believe what the states wanted, though," she said. "Both of them."

"Both of them? Two states?"

"It was in conjunction with a bridge," she explained, "and to *begin* with, they wanted both banks to look the same. Look bookends. They also wanted Astroturf and concrete trees."

"What do you mean, concrete trees?"

"I mean concrete trees. There are any number of concrete trees in America."

"The seeds must be something to look at. Where are these concrete trees?"

"Well, for instance, the palms in Palm Beach, Florida."

"They're concrete? The palm trees in Palm Beach aren't real? You're putting me on."

"No, I'm not," she promised. "Particularly along the main east-west boulevard—Avenue of the Palms, I think it's called."

"You *are* putting me on," I said, twisting around to look at her briefly *au naturel* rather than in the rearview mirror, because that kind of deadpan con-job hadn't seemed to be her style.

"You're telling me the palm trees on the Avenue of the Palms in Palm Beach are concrete, and you expect me to believe it."

"The real trees were knocked down or damaged in hurricanes," she told me. "The city fathers decided it would take too long to grow new trees, and besides another hurricane could knock down the new ones just as well, so they put up concrete palm trees instead. With plastic fronds."

"How do they look?"

"Real, unless you get right up close."

I looked around at the world with suddenly paranoid eyes. "You mean a lot of this stuff could be concrete?"

She laughed. "No, this is all too sloppy, it has to be real. And so's the park, by the way, we won our point there. No symmetry, no Astroturf, no concrete trees."

"What was their idea, anyway? Hurricanes?"

"Flood control. They wanted us to work with the Army Engineers, create a buffer so we'd have a strong flood abatement position right there at the bend in the river."

"What did they want to use for water?"

"We didn't ask. We just made a certain amount of fuss, and finally our opinion held sway."

"Good for you," I said, because although she kept using the pronoun 'we' I suspected from the ring of remembered battle in her voice that she'd been the primary figure on the good-guy side of the struggle.

"It was worth it," she said. "And the result is as mythic as you could hope for. With the Spanish moss on the *real* trees, and the broad slow river emphasizing the sweep of the bend, and the very flat banks extending well back with strong open spaces, it looks like something out of time. Prehistoric. That was the feeling we were trying for all along, the aura of pre-history, even of pre-man. An unhurried timelessness."

"Sounds very good."

"It was our feeling, too, what you said about the Mississippi having a mythic quality for Americans, and we wanted to represent that quality if we could. It seemed to us the Mississippi stands in the American mind for some sense of what the land used to be, long ago, before we came here and started making our mistakes."

"Like those," I said, pointing out some crumbling unpainted clapboard warehouses along the Illinois bank.

"There's so much left to be undone," she said. "But that could be beautiful along there, with a lot of time and patience."

"And money."

"The sad thing is," she said, "God did it right the first time, and didn't charge a cent."

## 13

By six-thirty, we were barely fifty miles into Missouri, with only four hundred on the day, but I was done in. After yesterday's six-hundred-mile dash, we were now just over a thousand miles from New York, about a third of the way, which was plenty. "Holiday Inn ahead," I called.

"What? Fine. You're ready to stop?"

"I've *been* ready to stop." It had been a grinding day.

"Oh. You should have said something."

"I've just been waiting for a Holiday Inn."

I had also been thinking about Holiday Inn, and yesterday's experiences, so as I took the exit ramp I said, "I have a suggestion, if you don't mind it."

"Try me."

"I'll wait in the car, while you go register."

"Fine," she said, as though she'd been privately thinking the same thing. "That would be simpler."

And so it was. She spent less than five minutes inside, then came out with a pair of keys and my instructions for driving around to our section of the building. Again we were on the second floor—up an outside staircase to the corridor—and again our doors were opposite one another. We agreed to meet at eight for dinner and I went into my room, *which was the same room.* I mean, the same room as last night, in Ohio. Same furniture in the same layout, same color scheme, same light fixtures, even the same pair of prints on the wall.

No, I can't say that, I can't be sure they were exactly the same elaborately framed prints hanging over the bed, because

I hadn't studied last night's; but the difference between fake Utrillos are so minor anyway that these were essentially the same even if they weren't. A curving uphill street in a Spanish town, chalky dusty street and buildings, a bit of red curtain in a dark slightly-out-of-focus window. That was one of tonight's entries; the other didn't have the bit of red curtain, but in a slightly-out-of-focus doorway it had what was either a sleeping child or a pile of laundry.

You can look at Holiday Inn art only so long, and soon I switched on and to the TV, settling down on the bed to watch the local news. You don't really get local news in New York, not in that hometown way, because New York is too big and indifferent to anybody's hometown, even if you were born there and live there without interruption all your life. For an automobile accident, say, to make it on New York's local news, it has to have taken place on the George Washington Bridge at rush hour, between a truckload of dynamite and a car driven by fleeing terrorists who've just kidnapped the Israeli ambassador. And sunk the bridge. In the sticks, for an automobile to make the TV news, all it has to do is hit something. Anything. A fire hydrant will do.

I was observing without much absorption a news item about high school band uniforms when there came a knock at the door. Killing the TV with a jab of my thumb, I went over to open the door and it was Katharine. She looked slightly worried, but trying to hide it, and she said, "Barry would like to talk to you."

"Barry?" I looked with some alarm down the hall. "Here?"

"On the phone, in my room. I called him."

"Oh. What's he want to talk about?"

"He just asked to speak to you."

Why was she looking so worried? "Okay," I said, and followed her across the hall. Her room was the same as mine, except the carpet and drapery colors had been reversed. It looked like the same ur-Utrillos on the wall, but I couldn't get close enough to be sure.

The phone—do they still call that shade of green 'avocado'? —had been moved with its long cord away from its normal home on the bedside stand over to the round Formica walnut-grain table by the window. I sat on the chair beside it, picked up the receiver, and said, "Hello?"

"Is that the driver?" He sounded less pleasant than when I'd overheard him with Katharine.

"That's right," I said.

"This is Barry Gilbert. I didn't catch your name."

I didn't throw it; well, you don't actually say that, do you? "Thomas Fletcher," I said.

"I've been following your route here, Fletcher," he said, "and it doesn't seem to me you're coming out the quickest way."

"Oh, no?"

"Why aren't you down on Interstate 40?"

"I don't have my maps here with me," I said. "They're in the cab. What's this Interstate 40?" And, listening to myself, I heard with some surprise that I was sounding more tough and more like your standard cabdrivuh than normal. I sounded, in fact, like my father. Now, why was I doing that?

"Interstate 40 is the most direct route," the bridegroom was saying. "Knoxville, Nashville, Memphis, Little Rock, Oklahoma City, Albuquerque, Flagstaff, right on into Los Angeles."

"Oh, yeah, I know the one you mean. I coulda dropped down on 81 from Pennsylvania, picked up 40 down south someplace." And from the corner of my eye I noticed Katharine now looking relieved, all worry gone. So that was it; she'd been afraid I wouldn't come across as the cliché cabdriver type she'd been claiming for me, that I'd sound too young or too educated and set off Barry's jealousy. So here we were in a conspiracy again, this time against her husband-to-be. Was this a healthy relationship?

Meanwhile, our victim was talking highways. "Here you are staying north," he said, "and there's no point in it, you'll only add extra mileage. Tell me something, Fletcher, just between you and me. I know you're not alone there, so all you have to do is say yes or no. Is this Miss Scott's idea?"

"No." *He* wasn't the one I was in the conspiracy with.

"Then I don't get it," he said. "I don't understand what you're doing on Route 70."

"Well, in the first place," I told him, "I'm driving the cab and you aren't even the customer. In the second place, it's summertime and the cab isn't air-conditioned, so I'd rather do St. Louis than Memphis. And in the third place, my route is just as short. I'll take 70 out to Utah, then drop down 15 to L.A., and it'll work out the same within a couple miles."

"Wait a minute, wait a minute." I could hear him rustling maps. "I see. I see. Down through Vegas."

"Right."

"Is that the idea, Fletcher? You want to see Vegas at somebody else's expense?"

"You work out the mileage, Mac," I told him. "And then I tell you what you do. You don't do any cab driving, and I don't do any face changing. Here's your intended." And I handed the phone to Katharine, saying, "If *I* was on my way to marry that guy, I'd go by tricycle."

"He's just upset," she said, sotto voce.

So was I. "Do I go criticize his noses?"

"I'll talk to you later, Tom." And into the phone she said, "Barry? Are you there?"

Of course he was there; hanging by his thumbs. So long as

he wasn't insulting my map-reading abilities—or my motivations: see Las Vegas at somebody else's expense indeed—I could sympathize with what the poor bastard was going through. How long must it have taken him to build up to this ultimatum? *Come out and get married right now, or forget the whole thing.* Scary. So finally he'd psyched himself up to it, he'd delivered the take-it-or-leave-it challenge, she'd agreed with him and accepted his terms, and what relief he must have felt knowing the suspense was finally over. And now here he was, with nothing resolved and the whole mess lasting an extra week. I too, in his position, might become a bit short-tempered, and might even take it out on an innocent bystander. Contenting myself with these thoughts—and also with the thought that I was *not* in Barry's position and not likely to be—I left Katharine stroking his fur in the right direction and returned to my own room and my TV, which was now concerning itself with the local sports scene.

You talk about fascinating.

## 14

Our route to the restaurant involved going outside again; down the exterior stairs and past our parked cab. A fiftyish couple was standing behind the cab as we went by, staring at it in complete astonishment. The woman was wearing broad-beamed pale green slacks, a pale green blouse with white polka dots, low-heel white shoes and a white cardigan sweater with little enlaced red-and-blue flowers around the neck and wrists. The man was dressed in white patent leather shoes, burgundy slacks, a narrow white patent leather belt, and an open-neck short sleeve shirt in broad vertical white-and-burgundy stripes. Both were short and stocky and big-nosed, and the man had a cigar in the corner of his mouth. As Katharine and I walked past, he took the cigar out of his face, pointed the wet end at the cab, and said to us, "This here is a New York City taxicab." *He* had the voice I'd been faking on the phone with Barry.

I said, "Oh?"

"I oughta know," he said.

He was prepared to tell us his life story—as though his appearance didn't proclaim it anyway—just because we happened to be passing by. If we admitted it was *our* New York City taxicab we'd be stuck with him the rest of our lives. "Ah," I said, therefore, took Katharine firmly by the elbow, and kept on walking.

Katharine glanced back over her shoulders, saying, quietly, "What was that all about?"

"That's a New York City taxicab *driver*," I told her. "On vacation."

She looked back again. "Are you sure?"

"No question. Visualize him in a cap."

"I see what you mean," she said, squinting. "That's why he said, 'I oughta know.' "

"Exactly."

We went on to the restaurant, which was called The Hills of Rome, and which was decorated as though we were inside one of them; the usual low-ceilinged broad cavern with heavily shrouded windows. Great fake-bronze bas reliefs of Caesarish individuals stared haughtily over our heads from all the walls, suggesting *they'd* know better than to eat here. And when we got our menus one section, headed "Roman Fare," was full of Neapolitan fare: meat and pasta drowned in tomato sauce. Fortunately, the rest of the menu was standard American.

The staff was entirely female, which meant they adapted much more readily to our circumstances. The headwaiter—maitresse d'?—took an absolute relish in going through the wine ritual with Katharine, then kept smiling toward our table from across the room.

Once the food and drink had been ordered, Katharine said, "I'm sorry about the way Barry talked to you."

"That's okay. The guy's under a certain amount of pressure."

"Thank you—for understanding."

And for pretending to be a plug-ugly on the phone; which neither of us would mention. "You're welcome," I said. "But maybe I shouldn't have any more chats with Barry."

"I'll do my best. Oh, and there's something else, a slight complication."

"Mm?"

"The man at the desk says Kansas City is two hundred miles from here. Could we get there by one-thirty tomorrow?"

"Easily. Why?"

"I phoned the office," she said, "and it turns out there's some paperwork I simply have to take care of. So they're flying a messenger to Kansas City in the morning; he'll be there a little after one, and we'll meet him at the airport."

All of which I found very impressive. Her talk about being a landscape architect and having business lunches and doing parks along the Mississippi had all been well and good, but I'd been visualizing it on rather a small scale. I have a cousin in Queens, on my mother's side, who's an interior decorator, working through various carpet outlets and furniture stores—when the shop says you can consult with "our trained decorator" they mean my cousin Myrna (born Mary)—so that's the way I'd been seeing Katharine's job. But nobody's going to fly a messenger to Kansas City to bring Myrna up to date on the paperwork; all at once I understood that Katharine wasn't fooling around. I was hanging out with a big gun. "You want the Kansas City airport at one-thirty," I told her, "that's what you're gonna get."

"Fine."

Food came then, and we ate in general silence, each thinking our own thoughts, until we had just the last bit of wine to dawdle over, when Katharine said, "There's another thing about tomorrow."

She made it sound ominous. I said, "Oh?"

"I keep thinking," she said, and paused, and watched her fingers turn the stem of her wineglass around and around and around. Still not looking up, she said, "I've been thinking that I don't absolutely *have* to use all this extra time. I *could* come to a decision before we reach Los Angeles."

"Sure," I said. "You could make up your mind any time at all."

"I've been going on the assumption I should give myself the whole week or five days or whatever it turns out to be, but when I talked to Frank tonight—"

"Frank?"

"My partner. At the office."

"Oh, right. He works late," I commented, because it had to have been eight o'clock New York time when she'd phoned.

"We tend to work late," she said, with a small smile. "Anyway, when I talked to him, I suddenly saw just how foolish this must look to an outsider. Taking a week out of your life to do nothing but mope about a decision. I make decisions every day."

"Of a different nature."

"Of a variety of natures," she said. "So I'm giving myself an earlier deadline. A kind of sub-deadline."

"Ah."

"I want to clear this up by the time we reach Kansas City," she said. "I want it settled in my mind by then, so if it's *yes* I can take a plane from there to Los Angeles, and if it's *no* I can take the flight back with the messenger."

A great depression settled down on me when she said that. I'd been enjoying this trip, enjoying her company. Was it going to end, less than halfway? I said, "If it's *no*, why take the plane back? I'll have to drive back anyway, why not ride along? Tomorrow's Saturday, you won't get any work done over the weekend anyway."

"Of course I will," she said. "I'm doing an atrium in Minneapolis, I haven't even done the preliminary sketches yet. Believe me, if I go back to New York tomorrow I'll have plenty to keep me occupied."

"Then *that's* the reason not to go."

Laughing, she said, "You're still recommending inaction, aren't you?"

"Nothing is usually the best thing to do."

"Not this time."

I very nearly said I'd miss her, but that wouldn't have been appropriate, would it? We'd become chummier over the last two days, but we were still nevertheless only employer and employee. Come to think of it, no matter what happened I would never know how the story came out; whatever plane she took tomorrow from Kansas City, the story surely wouldn't end there. Wouldn't she have more second thoughts in midflight, and land facing the opposite direction again? Obviously it all had to end sometime, if only because Barry was clearly not going to be able to play his role in the farce forever, but what the ending would be, and what would happen *after* the ending —because in life, of course, unlike stories, the only real ending is death—none of that would I ever learn. I was like a transient in a town, who goes to the local movie and sees Chapter Seven of a serial; I could dope out some of what had gone before, and I could make guesses about what would happen in later chapters, but Chapter Seven would remain the only part I actually *knew*.

While I brooded about all this, Katharine paid the check— her handwriting was large tonight when she added the tip— and we got up to go. I steered us slightly out of our way to bring us past the table at which the couple who'd been staring at the cab were now eating their desserts; banana split for him, butterscotch sundae for her. His cigar smoldered in the ash-tray, ready to his left hand. His clothing was still all burgundy and white, with white patent leather shoes. As we went by, I leaned down and said to him, "You wear that outfit in the Belmore Cafeteria, they'll think you're the soup of the day."

He looked up, startled, just beginning to get it as I quickly led Katharine on out of the restaurant. Outside, still looking back in a puzzled way, she said, "And what was *that* all about?"

"A local joke," I told her, and we walked back to our rooms.

## 15

I spent a depressed evening thinking about Katharine's latest decision. Would it all end tomorrow afternoon in *Kansas City*, of all places? The only ray of light in the gloom was that she hadn't made it definite. She'd called it a 'sub-deadline,' meaning she was already prepared to forgive herself if she didn't keep it. But what if she did? Drat.

By ten-thirty, the TV set and my own gloomy thoughts drove me to the outer darkness. Like a fool, I hadn't brought anything along to read, but would there be a magazine stand in the lobby?

There would not. But there would be a couple of paperback racks over near the desk; I brooded at them a while, finally realizing that among the variety of titles and covers I really only had three types of book to choose from. I could read a story in which a John Wayne-type hero saves the world or some portion of it from terrorists. Or I could read a 'historical' about a woman who loves a man despite—or because of—his cruelty. Or I could read a saga of four generations of a family; from farm to bank seemed to be the usual progression. I finally chose one of the sagas, primarily because I expected to be reading it in short bits at odd moments, and the saga would be the least likely to have a plot to remember. Also, all the characters in the saga would have the same last name, and I wouldn't have to wonder who they were every time I picked up the book.

But somehow I couldn't bring myself to go immediately back to the room and plunge directly into life on the old Gritbone farm. Next to the Hills of Rome restaurant was the Coliseum

Cocktail Lounge; tucking my saga into my hip pocket, I drifted in.

There didn't seem any particular reason to name this place after the Coliseum. In fact, *The Minepit* was about the only appropriate name I could think of for it. If it hadn't been for the light on the cash register, I might never have found the bar. The other illumination in the place consisted of six-watt blue bulbs deeply recessed in the dark ceiling. Black vinyl and dark walnut fake wood veneer covered most surfaces. It was brighter in the parking lot.

I climbed up on a massive stool and told the bartender-silhouette I'd like a beer. He mentioned two or three brands, and I mentioned back the one I hadn't immediately forgotten, and he brought me a small bottle, with a glass, and only charged a thousand dollars. Well, not quite that much.

As my eyes became more accustomed to the black, I became aware of two, or possibly three, other customers: all male, all solitary, all drinking beer. There was one at the end of the bar to my right, another one partway around the curve to my left, and I *think* there was one at a banquette behind me. There was no conversation, except the occasional murmur of a customer requesting a refill.

Could *any* family saga be worse than this? I was about to gulp down my beer and depart when someone else came in, stood at the bar to my right, and said, "Okay, Fred, here's the tabs."

A female voice. I looked over, and made out the profile of the headwaiter from next door. She handed a stack of checks to the bartender, then turned and saw me, smiled broadly, and said, "Hello, there."

"How you doing?"

"Long hard day," she said.

"Care for a drink?" It was the natural response, said prior to calculation.

She hesitated. I could see she'd like to say yes, but there was a question in her mind that first had to be resolved. She asked it: "Where's your friend?"

"Up in her room." Then I said, "*You* know she and I aren't hanging out together."

She slid onto the stool next to me. "To tell the truth, I was fascinated by you two."

"It's a long story. Sure you won't have a drink?"

She peered in the dimness at the glass and bottle in front of me. "What's that? Beer? I can't drink beer, it goes right to my hips. I have to watch my girlish figure."

She did have a girlish figure, as a matter of fact, long and rangy, and a long rangy face. She was about my age, maybe a couple years older. She wasn't a beauty, but she was attractive; rather like the younger women in the family saga in my hip pocket, I supposed. I said, "They'll serve you anything you want here, it's a regular joint. Right, Fred?"

"Sure," said the Fred-silhouette. I still hadn't seen his face, didn't know if he ever smiled or frowned or anything, but his voice sounded friendly enough.

"Then I'll have a Scotch and water," she said. "My name's Sue Ann, by the way."

"Hi, Sue Ann, I'm Tom." And we shook hands; hers was long-fingered and hard-boned and cool.

Our first topic of conversation was the relationship between Katharine and me, which took a while to describe, with several detours. For instance: "Oh, that's *your* taxi out there! I recognized it right away for a New York cab. I lived in New York three years."

"Oh, yeah?"

"My ex-husband was in construction," she said. "He worked on the World Trade Center. We had a nice house on Staten Island; off Drumgoole Boulevard, you know that section?"

"Not really."

"We used to go up to Manhattan all the time. Go to the movies on Broadway, or some nice Italian restaurant in the Village. Do you know Rocco's, down on Thompson Street?"

"Afraid not."

"Great Italian food." And she leaned close, resting her hand on my forearm and speaking confidentially. "Not like this place." Then she straightened again, saying, "But how come your passenger's taking a taxi all the way out here?"

"Further than here," I said, and went on to explain Katharine's destination and motive. Sue Ann's reaction was immediate: "Tell her forget it. Anybody plans to get married, my advice is, shoot yourself instead. It's quicker."

"You've been burned, huh?"

"You know it, brother. How about you?"

"A little scorched around the edges," I acknowledged.

She studied me, as best she could in the cash register light. "You don't look married," she decided.

"I'm not married, not anymore."

She lifted her glass. "Mazel tov." She knocked back some more of her drink, then said, "I learned that word in New York."

"Oh, yeah."

"It's Greek. It means 'congratulations'."

Correct her? Definitely not. "Then mazel tov, yourself," I said. "I take it you left your husband on top of the World Trade Center?"

"With that other giant ape," she said, and broke herself up laughing. She was a good old girl. When the laughing fit eased, she said, "You know what broke the camel's back?"

"The last straw," I suggested.

"That's what I'm gonna tell you." One of us was getting a little drunk. "Ralph's car was towed away. You know they do that in New York? Park in the wrong place, they tow your car away."

"That can be expensive," I said.

"Sixty-five dollars," she told me, "just to get your car back. And that doesn't count the parking ticket. But *also* you know what they do? They keep records, they check to see are there any unpaid *old* parking tickets on that car, they don't let you have the car back until you pay up."

"Ralph had some old tickets, huh?"

She leaned close again, speaking with slow emphasis. "Four-hun-dred-dol-lars." Then she grinned sidelong, and added, "You never saw anybody so mad in your in-tie-er life."

"I bet."

"It was when I laughed he slugged me. So I went and got Jason's bat and—"

"Jason?"

"Ralph's son from a previous marriage. Ralph's the marrying kind. Jason's OK, he's about fourteen now. Anyway, I went and got his baseball bat and snuck up behind Ralph while he was getting a beer out of the refrigerator, and I gave him a shot he's *still* feeling." She laughed again, and tried to drink from her glass, and discovered it was empty.

"We need refills." I turned to wave at the Fred-silhouette.

"My round," Sue Ann said, and when Fred came over she told him, "Again, Fred. On my tab. Or, wait a minute." To me, she said, "You want to stick to beer? It'll bloat you all up."

"Well, I don't know," I said. "I had gin before dinner, wine with dinner, and now beer. How do you suggest I round it off?"

"With a stinger," she said. "Definitely."

"Hey, look, lady. I have to drive tomorrow."

"Two stingers, Fred," she said. "And don't go too heavy with the ice."

"I gotta close up in a few minutes, Sue Ann."

"That's okay, we'll drink fast."

"I seem to be getting a stinger," I said, as the Fred-silhouette went away.

"You know," she said, "you're a good guy."

"I am?"

"For instance, the way you handled yourself at dinner. You didn't try to take over, and you didn't make a big fuss about *not* taking over. You know what burns my ass?"

"No, I don't."

"The birthday wives. In comes a couple, it's her birthday so she doesn't have to cook, and they shoved the kids off onto Aunt Sadie, and now they've got this idea *she'll* take *him* to dinner out of her birthday money. So they sit there, and she blushes and giggles and she's all helpless, and she about faints when it's time to taste the wine—half a bottle of Blue Nun, you'd think it was the end of the world. And the *husband* sits there with this big fat-headed smile on his face, being *proud* of the little lady. It's *exactly* like birthday teenagers, thirteen-year-old kids getting to order their own dinner for the first time, with the grown-ups all smiling at each other, isn't-it-sweet, how-time-flies, all that malarkey. But here you've got the same thing with a forty-five-year-old woman, she's off the leash for one day in her life. I tell you, Tom, there's more than once I've wished I had Jason's baseball bat."

"For the husband, or the wife?"

She thought that over for a few seconds, and then nodded. "You're right. For both of them."

Meantime, the bar's other customers had drifted on out of the joint, our stingers had been delivered and tasted—deceptively gentle and cool little devils—and now Fred started ringing up all the tabs on his cash register. You know the way they do: ba-*bring*-a, *bring*-a, *bring*-a, on each and every check covering each and every transaction of that business day. The noise is loud, repetitive, interminable, and intolerable. "Jesus," I said. "What a racket."

"He's got to do it, Tom," Sue Ann told me. Her loyalty was, after all, on Fred's side of the bar. "He can't go home until he's rung them all up."

"Well, I can. Why don't we finish these drinks in the lobby?"

"*You* might be able to get away with that," she said, "but I wouldn't. Remember, I work here."

"Then come up to my room. We can borrow the glasses, can't we?"

"Sure we can." But she hesitated, looking at me with a slightly crooked grin, before finally giving an abrupt nod and saying, "Yeah, let's get out of here, it's too loud." She yelled a good night to Fred over the clanging of his cash register, and we left the Coliseum forever.

The evening air, as we walked from the lobby around to the side stairs, was cool and crisp, but it didn't do much for the mush that seemed to have gotten into my brain. I was thinking clearly enough—for instance, I knew damn well that Sue Ann and I were on our way to bed together—but my normal activities, such as walking and talking, were all a bit slurred and shambly. I hoped not all my abilities had been impaired by drink.

Upstairs, I had an oddly uncomfortable feeling about Katharine's door; it seemed to disapprove of me, though there was no reason why it should. There was nothing between Katharine and me. If I was going behind anybody's back it was Rita's, my occasional roommate back in New York, and she couldn't have cared less. Nevertheless, I hunched my shoulders against the imagined emanations from Katharine's door as I unlocked my own.

Once inside my room, all that nonsense disappeared without trace. Sue Ann said, "Christ, all these rooms look alike, don't they?" In response, I took her drink out of her hand, placed both glasses atop the low dresser, put my arms around her and kissed her.

Nice. Nice soft moving mouth, nice tongue, good lean rangy body slender and muscular beneath my hands. It *had* been a while, by golly. "Bed," I murmured, against her lips.

"Mm, yes."

Lovely. Sex is so nice, exploring that other body, rolling together, the terrific physical sensations, the wonderful things that can be done with mouths, hands, fingers—with all sorts of body parts, combining in so many soft sweet ways. And my abilities had *not* been impaired; that was also nice.

Afterwards, we lay side by side on the sheets and sipped our stingers. Sue Ann was a smoker, so she had the ritual cigarette. Puffing on it, squinting through the smoke, she said, "That was the one nice thing about marriage. The regular fucking. I did like that."

A smell of darkroom chemicals seemed to waft past my nose, competing with Sue Ann's low-tar fumes. "Sometimes even that was a mixed blessing," I said.

She gave me a sympathetic knowing smile. "You bet your life. Lemme tell you a joke."

"Sure."

"The point isn't so much the joke," she said, "as the guy who told it and how the other guys took it."

"Fire away."

"I was working in a diner, before I got the job here, and every morning we'd get these salesmen in, same bunch of boys, come in for an hour from maybe nine to ten. Supposed to be out making sales, they'd come in and kill some time together instead. Told a *lot* of jokes. They loved jokes, those boys, and they'd laugh and roll around and spill their coffee and have a great old time. Except this one joke. Seems this couple went to the zoo, they went to see the big gorilla, and the wife started teasing the gorilla, sticking her tongue out at him, and wiggling her behind at him and all that stuff. And the husband kept saying, 'Myrtle, don't do that, you're getting the gorilla all upset.' But she kept on anyway, and the gorilla *was* getting upset, and all at once the gorilla *yanked* those bars apart and *jumped* through and grabbed Myrtle up and ran off with her. And naturally Myrtle was screaming, and her husband ran along after them, and he shouted, 'Myrtle! Tell him you've got a headache!' "

"Ah," I said.

"Right." She had a very fetching, very sexy crooked grin. "None of those salesmen actually *laughed* at that joke. They more growled at it. They all said, '*Yeaa*-uh.' And that, mister, is all I know about marriage."

I said, "You don't have a headache now, do you?"

"What? Well, look at *you*," she said.

## 16

Somebody was shaking my shoulder. Opening my eyes I saw a breast impending close above me, and heard a knocking in the middle distance at the same time a voice said, "Somebody's at the door."

Voice = Sue Ann = memory = explanation of breast. Nice breast. I reached for it, and my shoulder was shaken more roughly, Sue Ann saying more urgently, "*Some*-body's knocking at the *room door*."

"Yes," I said, sitting up, trying to simulate alertness. I found the perimeter of the bed—Holiday Inn beds are wonderfully large, large enough for anything—from there reached the floor without too much difficulty, rose on those shillelaghs that once were my legs, tottered across the room, and remembered just before reaching the still knock-knocking door that I was nude. So I stood behind it as I sliced it open a crack, and peered around the edge at Katharine, whose face displayed an intricate balance of annoyance and concern. Knowing at once what the problem was, I of course asked the unnecessary question: "What time is it?"

"Ten after nine." Now that she'd seen I was still alive and capable of both walking and talking, she was becoming much less concerned and much more annoyed.

"Oh." I tried to find my brains, so I could cudgel them. A brain without cudgel is like a cake without yeast; nevertheless I attempted to rise to the occasion, saying, "I forgot to leave a call."

"We have to get to Kansas City," she reminded me, "by one-thirty."

"Right. Right. Where are you, in the restaurant?"

"I *was*."

"I'll meet you there, in five minutes."

While Katharine said something else about the urgency of the situation—she was letting off irritation, and had every right —I glanced back toward the bed, where Sue Ann was grinning foxily at me. Women love to see a man nagged by another woman.

Sexy grin. Sexy woman. Sue Ann looked very very good. So I'd drive faster. "Make it fifteen minutes," I said, and shut the door.

## 17

Katharine was *very* annoyed. "It's been almost half an hour."

"Coffee," I said, to the hovering waitress, and sat down.

Katharine gave me a critical evaluation: "You were drinking last night."

"I think maybe the pork chops were bad."

"They were not. I phoned your room around eleven, and you weren't there."

What crap was this? After Sue Ann, who had been a lot of very uncomplicated fun, who needed a harridan taking liberties she hadn't earned? *We* weren't shacked up. "Look, lady," I said. "You hired me to drive the cab. I didn't hire you to cure me of my vices."

"Yes, your vices," she said, and all at once she wasn't really annoyed anymore. Looking at her, it seemed to me she was actually amused. Did she know I'd been with a woman last night? How do women do that sort of thing? All at once they *know*.

My coffee came while I was still trying to work out a response. There was none, though, so I busied myself with milk and sugar.

Katharine, in yet a different tone, said, "Have some breakfast."

"We're late."

"You need the protein." Was that another smart crack? To the waitress she said, "Bring the gentleman a number three." Then, to me, "Orange juice or grapefruit juice."

"Grapefruit." I needed the shock to my system.

"And he likes his eggs over easy."

"No, I don't think so," I said. "This morning, in honor of myself, I think I better have them scrambled. Makes them easier to deal with."

After the waitress went away, I said, "What were you phoning for, last night?"

"I wanted to know if you play chess. I have a travel set."

"Oh. No, I don't, not really. I fooled around with it in college, that's all." Then, because her earlier manner still rankled, I said, "It isn't among my vices."

"Now, don't get bad-tempered," she said. "I didn't get mad at you when you called me *look-lady*."

"Well, why should you?"

"Tom," she said, "wait just a minute. Let's start all over again. You're a little hungover this morning, and I've been very edgy because I want to make my decision by the time we get to Kansas City, and we're *very* close to having a fight."

"I'm not starting anything," I said, grumpily, then immediately heard my own words and regretted them. "No, forget that. You're right, we're both a little touchy this morning."

"Friends?" She extended her hand across the table.

"Friends," I agreed, and took her hand, which was smaller and more delicate than Sue Ann's. (Flashback: Complete physical recall of Sue Ann.)

The waitress returned with my grapefruit juice, my side order of toast, and a plate containing number three: scrambled eggs and ham. I ate, more doggedly than enthusiastically, meantime thinking about one thing and another, including the idea of Katharine phoning me at eleven at night to play chess. Was that possible? Could it be I'd had my choice of *two* women last night? I couldn't believe it, but I paused in my protein-harvesting to ask the question: "What made you want to play chess last night?"

An ironic smile played like heat lightning on her lips. "I'm not one of your vices either," she said. "I was getting very nervous and depressed, that's all, thinking about Barry and Kansas City and everything, and sometimes it helps to distract yourself with a game. That's all there was to it, Tom." She was looking very serious now. "I thought we understood one another, that's why I felt I could call."

"We do understand one another."

"I'm not in the market for an affair," she said. "Nor a one-night stand. Not with anybody. Don't you think I've thought about it?"

"No," I said, in some surprise.

"It's the worst solution to my problem," she said. "The way to deal with the question by making it obsolete."

"I see what you mean." And I did; she hadn't meant she'd thought about having an affair with *me*, she meant she'd thought about having an affair, period. With anybody, just to cop out on the Barry decision. And she was too smart to let it happen that way.

I finished my breakfast and we separated, her to pay the bill, me to get the luggage from both rooms and stash it all in the cab. Sue Ann was gone from the room, leaving in her wake the mingled aromas of sex, cigarette smoke, and shower steam; I gave the bed a grateful smile on the way by.

The family saga that had brought us together was on the floor. I shoved it into my suitcase, got Katharine's things from across the way—what a neat person she was—put everything in the trunk of the cab, and drove around front. When I went in to leave the keys at the desk, Katharine was just finishing, and we started out together. Katharine said, deadpan, out of the corner of her mouth, "The headwaiter wants you."

I looked over at the restaurant entrance, and there was Sue

Ann, looking demure and foxy. She gave me a grin and a tiny nod of the head and a one-finger wave from down at her side.

*I must stop off here on the way back.* I returned her smile, and Katharine and I went out to the cab. As I held the rear door for her, she gave me a sidelong look and said, "I'm glad I gave her a good tip."

## 18

Noon, and we were still eighty miles from Kansas City. Our late start had been complicated by my hangover, which made me slightly jittery and awkward, so that I drove more slowly than usual. But the protein Katharine had insisted I shovel in was beginning to take effect, and time itself was engaged in its legendary healing process, so I was steadily feeling more human.

As for Katharine, my occasional glances in the rearview mirror showed her suffering the deadline whim-whams once more. Talking to herself, looking agitated, brushing her hands back through her hair; all the symptoms I remembered from that first day on the way to Kennedy airport were once again in evidence, and getting stronger. It was on the way to being a total relapse.

The countryside was flatter here than it had been east of the Mississippi. Square or rectangular fields of corn and wheat and other growing things—I'm no farmer, I wouldn't know a rutabaga from a rapscallion—were spread in undulating neatness in all directions, under a sun so high and clear it was like a growing-lamp hung in the sky by the Department of Agriculture. The sky itself was a cloudless pale blue, rising to a deeper blue at the horizon. I'm sorry, but the sky *was* like a bowl and the green-and-tan land *was* like a checkerboard. Some of those archetypal descriptions just can't be bettered.

Gas was getting low. The trademarks for Chevron and Mobil were red-white-and-blue kites anchored in the sky far ahead; I eased into the right lane, took the exit, and chose one of them. "And check the oil," I told the kid in the Kansas City Chiefs sweatshirt.

He gawped at me. "This here's a New York City taxicab, isn't it?"

"Yes, it is."

"You're sure a long way from home."

"You bet."

He went off, shaking his head, to fill the tank and check the oil, and I turned around to say, "Katharine."

She looked at me in an impatient distracted way; I was keeping her from poking at the sore tooth. "What?"

"Come sit up front."

"Why?"

"We'll talk."

At first, this suggestion seemed only to annoy her. She shook her head irritably, turning away to frown out her window at the gas pumps, then looked back with a quizzical expression, studied my face, thought it over, and said, "Thank you, Tom. You're right."

While she was transferring I cleared the front seat of road-maps—some went on the dash, some got stuck down between seat and door—and when she slid in next to me she already looked less upset, though she had nothing to say.

Fewer gas stations are on credit cards—other than their own—since the Arab oil crunch. Once again Katharine had to pay cash, and when the boy brought back the change he said to me, "How far you goin?"

"Los Angeles."

"Started in New York?"

"Sure."

"You're gonna be awful mad if I tell you," he said. He was smirking, looking very amused about something.

Wasn't Los Angeles there anymore? Perhaps it had finally fallen into the sea, during an earthquake, while a great Voice spake from Heaven, and It cryeth: *"Enough! No more tacky!"* I said, "Go ahead, tell me."

He leaned close through the window; it was time he changed his sweatshirt. Confidential, keeping his voice too low for the passenger to hear, he said, "You forgot to turn your meter on."

"Well, son of a gun," I said, looking at the meter in question. Then I shrugged and said, "The heck with it. Too late now. Thanks, though." As I drove away, the boy's smirk was just beginning to turn puzzled.

Well, Katharine was up front with me, but she didn't immediately turn into a chatterbox. We got back onto Route 70, eased gradually up to seventy-five miles an hour, and I said, "Penny for your thoughts."

"I wish I was married," she said.

I glanced at her profile, which was very very gloomy. "You mean already married, decisions over and done with?"

"No. I wish I'd been married before, like you. So I'd know more about it now."

"You could have been married ten times before," I pointed out, "and you still wouldn't know what marriage with *Barry* would be like."

"Still."

Which pretty well short-circuited the conversation for a few minutes, until I asked her a question that had been in my mind several times the last couple of days: "How come you *haven't* been married?"

"What? Well—it just never happened."

"Phooey. What are you, twenty-eight?"

"Thirty," she said, with a little smile.

"People have asked you to marry them," I said. "Before Barry."

"Actually, not so much," she said. "I don't know how things were in the old days, but in my case men mostly asked me to move in with them." She was relaxing a bit more, now that she was talking; scrunching down in the seat, she said, "My sophomore year in college I lived with a boy. His name was Andy."

"Did *he* ask you to marry him?"

"Yes. At the end of the year. He was a senior, and he was graduating and going to the University of Virginia for his Master's. He wanted me to go with him, and he said why don't we get married?"

"And you said?"

"I said I don't want to get married."

"You wanted to finish college."

"Well, partly." Then she giggled, a surprising sound, and said, "Can I tell you something silly?"

"I'm sure you can."

"It was the refrigerator," she said.

"The refrigerator."

"Andy's mother," she explained, "was one of those crazy Tupperware ladies, everything in her life inside a plastic Tupperware container with the lid on it and a label glued to it, and stuck in the refrigerator. And Andy was the same way. She used to *mail* him Tupperware. Empty Tupperware containers, for his own use. The Parcel Post man would come with a package, and we'd open it up, and here's this Tupperware. And inside it there's another one, and another one inside *that*. And the last one empty."

"I can see where this isn't particularly romantic," I said, "but I don't get the connection with why you didn't want to marry him."

"I hate leftovers."

"Oh."

"I didn't originally, but I do now. I have ever since. Our refrigerator was *full* of leftovers. But Andy wasn't neat like his mother, he didn't put labels on things, he just put them all in the refrigerator, saying he'd 'remember.' And a true Tupperware person, you know, never takes anything *out* of a Tupperware container, that defeats the whole purpose. After a while, I just hated to even *think* about the refrigerator."

"It got full, huh?"

"It got scary. The things I could identify—like half a slice of toast, and I'm not kidding—those were bad enough, but the real killers were the things you couldn't recognize at all. Every once in a while I'd go through what I called an Anonymous Reject Day. I'd pick a time when Andy was in class, and I'd take six or seven of the oldest and most anonymous Tupperwares out of the refrigerator and *throw them away*."

"Wouldn't he notice the empties?"

"You don't understand me," she said. "Do you think I was going to *open* those things, *touch* what was inside? When I say I threw them away, I mean I *threw* them *away*."

"Ah hah."

"It was the only way to leave enough room for milk and eggs."

"And Andy never caught on."

"Never."

"But when he asked you to marry him and go live in Virginia—"

"All I could see was that refrigerator, for the rest of my life. I couldn't face it."

"Absolutely understandable."

"And the thing is," she said, half turning toward me, being very solemn and serious, "the thing is, in every other way Andy was terrific. He was very bright, and he had a good sense of humor, and he respected my individuality, and…um. I don't know how to say this."

"He was good in bed."

She sighed. "If you mention sex in front of a man, he thinks you're offering some."

"Exception noted."

"Not that I have any desire to go into the gory details," she assured me. "But, yes, Andy was the first guy I ever slept with that I had a really wonderful time. I'd had some sexual experiences before—not many—but it had been fun and that's all. You know? Like dancing."

"Got it."

"I learned a lot from Andy." Grinning in lascivious reminiscence, she said, "We learned a lot from one another."

"If you keep leering like that," I said, "I'll tell you about *my* experiences."

"Oh, I'm sorry. I'm being provocative."

"Somebody is. Anyway, with Andy, Tupperware was stronger than sex."

"Absolutely."

"It seems to me," I said thoughtfully, "just from that one experience you already have a pretty good idea what marriage is."

"I think you're being cynical," she said.

"You said Andy was every other way perfect."

"I said terrific; that's not quite perfect."

"Okay, terrific. But you had to live with the guy, in a marital kind of situation, to know what he was really like for *you*. So it's the same thing with Barry, isn't it?"

"Hardly," she said. "Barry and I *have* slept together, you know."

"I guessed."

"We've lived together, too, on and off."

"How much on, how much off?"

"What?"

Had she thought that a sexual reference? "How much time

in the last two years," I rephrased it, "have you spent living together?"

"Oh. I don't know exactly. A week or two here, a week or two there. Last year I spent six weeks in California on a job, and I lived with Barry almost the entire time. And he's lived with me in New York, and we've shared hotel rooms in different places. There aren't any Tupperware surprises ahead of me with Barry, if that's what you mean."

"Okay. Then the question is, what's holding you back?"

She looked at me with troubled eyes. "That's the question, all right," she said.

## 19

There are two Kansas Citys, and therefore there are two Kansas City airports. The one in Kansas City, Kansas is called Fairfax Municipal Airport, and the one in Kansas City, Missouri is called Kansas City Municipal Airport. They are diagonally across the Missouri River from one another, and neither of them was the one we wanted.

Which we learned when we pulled in at Kansas City Municipal Airport in Kansas City, Missouri. It seems there was *another* airport, called Kansas City International Airport, over on the Kansas side, about twelve or fifteen miles north of *all* the Kansas Citys, along Interstate Route 29. (We'd already passed an East Kansas City and a North Kansas City on our way into town; you could get pretty sick of that name after a while. "If I ever see *The Wizard of Oz* again," I told Katharine, "I'm going to root for the tornado.")

Since it was already after one o'clock when we reached the wrong airport, Katharine phoned ahead to the right one, leaving the messenger a message; then we picked our way through the supermarkets and used-car lots and machine-parts shops in overgrown clapboard garages out onto Interstate 29 and ran north to something called Ferrelview. Not knowing what a ferrel is, I can't say whether or not we viewed it, but that was also the exit for the airport, a sprawling sunbaked assemblage of stucco and asphalt, where the plane from the east had long since landed and no one had given the messenger the message.

And now I saw Katharine the executive at work. When her first enquiry at the Information counter got her nothing but smiling bewilderment from the friendly mindless girl on duty there, Katharine smiled coldly back and said, "Your supervisor, please."

"Ma'am, I've been on duty here the last three hours, and there hasn't been any such message."

"Since I'm the one who phoned it in," Katharine said, "I do know it exists. Your supervisor, please."

The girl, not delighted, went away. Katharine stood fuming, passing her attaché case from hand to hand. Trying to relax her, I said, "Things never do run smoothly."

"Oh, yes, they do," she said.

In about three minutes the girl herself came back, with an envelope. "It hadn't been sent down," she said, rather snippily, and handed the envelope to Katharine.

Looking over Katharine's shoulder, I saw it was some sort of standard message form, and that it was addressed *to* Katharine Scott. "Arriving soon, reserve office. Messenger, Willson, Garfield & Co." I stepped a pace to one side, wanting a clear view of the explosion.

But she didn't explode. Refolding the message, she said, more quietly than ever, "Your supervisor, please."

"Well, that's the message, isn't it?"

"Your *super*-visor, please."

The girl's attention had been belatedly caught. Looking a bit worried, she said, "If you'll tell me what's wrong, Madam, I'm certain we can—"

"Are you refusing to call your supervisor?"

The girl thought about that one for maybe six seconds, then her face closed down into a total defensive stolidity and she picked up a phone from under her counter. She spoke briefly, then hung up and pointedly turned to the person on line behind us, who wanted to know about direct flights to Nashville.

Nashville? When you're in Kansas City, what's the point in going to Nashville?

The supervisor arrived promptly, and was a mid-fortyish stocky woman with a thick black skirt and a no-nonsense manner. "Is there something you don't understand, Madam?"

"I don't understand how anybody can be so stupid," Katharine answered.

The woman blinked. "Madam?"

"This message." Katharine handed it over, and while the woman looked at it Katharine said, "The *first* stupidity is that the girl here insisted the message didn't exist. It was only when I asked to speak to you that she went looking for it."

"Yes, I see," the woman said. "Well, it was found, wasn't it? And you wanted to reserve an office?"

"I want to talk about the second stupidity," Katharine told her. "You'll see it's addressed to me."

"Is your name spelled wrong? Sometimes over the phone—"

"*And* you'll see it's from a messenger from Willson, Garfield and Company."

"Madam, I'm sorry, I don't understand the complaint. True, there was a breakdown, it took a *few extra moments* to deliver the message—"

"I sent it," Katharine said.

The woman looked blank. "I'm sorry," she said. "What was that?"

"I sent the message. *I* sent the message *to* the messenger from Willson, Garfield and Company, who got off the plane from New York—" she consulted her watch "—twenty-five minutes ago and is by now God knows where."

The woman was thunderstruck. "This message isn't for you?"

"This message is *from* me. You have not only lost my message, you have lost my messenger." She looked at her watch again—for effect, no doubt. "And how much longer do you intend to keep me standing here before you find my messenger?"

The woman opened her mouth, closed it, looked at the message still in her hand, looked at Katharine, and stepped briskly to the Information counter, shunting aside the Nashville-bound person with a no-nonsense hip. "Did anyone from Flight six-two-three leave a message here, or ask for a message?"

The girl's reaction time was too slow for longterm survival. This was the moment to stop being sullen and start expressing all kinds of helpfulness, but she missed it. Face still closed, she told her own immediate superior, "I'm sure I don't know."

"We'll see about *that*, Miss. Give me the phone."

Too late, the girl noticed that the signals had changed. Quickly producing the phone, she said, "I don't *remember* anybody. Should I go through all the messages?"

"Continue with this other gentleman," the woman said, gesturing at our friend from Nashville. Then, with briskly efficient fingers, she dialed a three-digit number, spoke briefly, read off the message, listened to a response, spoke again, and broke the connection. Another three-digit number was dialed, and an even briefer conversation took place, during which the public address system suddenly announced: "Will the messenger from Willson, Garfield and Company go to the main Information Desk? Will the messenger from Willson, Garfield and Company go to the main Information Desk, please?"

Her phoning done, the woman turned to Katharine and said, "I'm terribly sorry about this, Madam. If you'll come with me, I have the office reserved." Then, turning back to the girl, she said, "When the messenger arrives, have him escorted at once to conference room six."

"Yes, certainly," the girl said. "I'll do it myself."

"Yes, do that. And then come see me."

Leaving the girl with her eyes and mouth blinking like a fish in an aquarium, the woman led us away, across the polished composition floor and up a flight of stairs and through an unmarked white door, all the while apologizing for the mix-up. Beyond the white door was a white corridor, flanked by doorways, each revealing a conference room containing a long oval table surrounded by leatherette chairs.

Ours—a black metal 6 was screwed to the white door—was midway down the right side. Showing us in, the woman said, "I'm sure the messenger will be along very shortly."

Katharine looked around. "Is there a phone?"

"Certainly, Madam, right here." And she picked it up from a stand to one side and moved it with its long cord over to the conference table. "You dial nine for an outside line, then give the number to the operator."

Katharine had opened her attaché case on the table and brought out pen and legal pad. "May I have your name and extension?"

The woman hesitated, but had no choice: "I'm Mrs. Fairborne. One twenty-seven." Watching Katharine write it down, she said, "I intend to speak severely to that young lady."

"She isn't the one who *took* the message."

"Oh, I'll certainly look into that as well. It's so hard to find reasonably competent people these days."

"That's why competent supervision is so important," Katharine said.

Mrs. Fairborne didn't like that. "Yes, of course," she said. "Well, I have no doubt everything will be all right now. If there's any problem, just get right in touch with me."

"Thank you, I will."

Mrs. Fairborne bowed herself out, closing the door very

gently, and I grinned at Katharine, saying, "You're tough."

"You have to be," she said, still grim-faced. Then she shook her head, as though forcing herself into a different gear. "As a matter of fact, you do have to be," she said. "A woman does. A woman has to be *much* tougher than a man if she's going to be taken seriously."

"I suppose that's true."

Seating herself at the end of the oval table, she pulled her open attaché case closer, then glanced into it and seemed very troubled by something she saw there. "Barry," she said, and gave me a helpless look.

"No decision, huh?"

"Well, how *can* I?" She was being very irritable now. "The whole *idea* of this trip was to get *away* from scenes like this, have some leisurely time to myself, to think things out without interruption."

"That's right."

"Well, how can I think in this atmosphere? Doing that woman's job for her. If she's the supervisor, let her supervise."

"There's still the original plan," I said. "Another three, four days to Los Angeles."

"I'd so wanted to get everything resolved *now*. I hate being indecisive. You probably find that hard to believe, but you're seeing me in a very unusual light."

"I'd already figured that out," I assured her.

"Normally I'm very decisive, very sure of myself." She took a deep breath, gripping the edge of the table, and let it forcefully out. "Think," she told herself. "It's time to get your head together."

I sat midway along the table and watched her frown at the walnut-grain formica top. With her jaw clenched, her facial bone structure was rather more pronounced; she had beautiful cheekbones. I had a sudden urge to kiss her. I did *not* make that mistake.

There was a knock at the door. "Puff," Katharine said, letting air out again, sagging in a defeated way, and I got up to open the door.

The messenger was a surprise. I'd expected some skinny kid, but he was probably in his late forties, hair very gray and rather long and unkempt, face jowly and thick-featured, body out of shape and tending to fat. He wore a thin darkish tie, a medium-gray and rather shabby suit, a wrinkled white shirt, ordinary black shoes, and hornrim glasses. He was carrying an attaché case like Katharine's, only thicker. He looked like a not very successful druggist. What was he doing being a messenger?

He looked at me. "Katharine Scott?"

"No," I said, and pointed. "That's her there."

He already knew her. "Afternoon, Miss Scott," he said, coming in.

She smiled at him, in a brisk impersonal way. "Hello, Roy. Sorry about the mix-up."

"Oh, that's okay, Miss Scott."

I closed the door and returned to my seat. Roy didn't sit down, nor did Katharine ask him to. Putting his attaché case on the table near hers, he opened it and withdrew a thin sheaf of papers. "This is the presentation on the Mall," he said. "Mr. Willson said you wanted to go over it before copies were run off."

"Oh, yes. Fine."

For the next fifteen minutes or so, I sat there and watched Katharine play executive, while Roy stood attentively at her side, handing her papers, taking papers back, occasionally writing down on a memo pad instructions she would give him, such as, "Tell Henry to leave the people *out* of the drawing.

This isn't an automobile ad, it's an architectural presentation." And, "Tell Frank I just don't think we can deal with those people. I've met them three times, and they're simply not serious in terms of cost. All they really want to do is plant a few rhododendron and look the other way. If Frank wants to pursue it, that's up to him, but he should *certainly* not tender any suggestions." Each time, Roy nodded and wrote it all down in what seemed to be shorthand, and at the end he took the last papers back, put them with the memo pad into his attaché case, closed it, and said, "Thank you, Miss Scott."

"Thank *you*, Roy." Katharine got to her feet and stretched. "What time is your flight back?"

"Three-twenty."

She looked at her watch. My own was still in the cab, but I estimated it was now a bit after two-thirty. I saw Katharine look thoughtful for a few seconds; then she glanced over at me with a rueful expression, and said to Roy, "Have a good flight."

"Thanks, Miss Scott."

"Nice to meet you," I said, getting to my feet, as he turned toward the door.

He nodded to me, with a noncommittal expression, and left. At no point had he shown the slightest curiosity about anything; not about me, or what Katharine was doing, or anything else.

"Well," Katharine said, with a happy smile. "*That's* a relief."

Meaning she wouldn't have to think about the office anymore. But I knew what the *real* relief was; she'd put off the decision yet again.

Looking over at me, she said, "On to Los Angeles?"

"Sure," I said.

She frowned. "Something's wrong."

"No, there isn't."

"Yes, there is. Something's wrong."

"We're wasting time," I said. "On to Los Angeles." And I held the door open.

She went on frowning at me a moment longer, then shrugged and picked up her attaché case. "Have it your own way."

"There's nothing wrong," I insisted. There was, of course; but I didn't want to talk about it.

# 20

All airports make you drive in great circles to get anywhere. You can never just drive *in* to the airport and then turn around and drive back *out* again. You have to loop over and under and in and out and through and around, all on a network of roads architecturally based on the concept of the Christmas-present bow, following endless barely comprehensible signs. I had hardly begun this unreeling process when a cop stepped out in front of me and flagged me down. When I came to a stop, he trod over to my window and said, "Didn't you see the sign back there?"

"I saw about six hundred signs back there. Which one did you have in mind?"

"The one that said no commercial traffic," he told me. "The one that said taxis to the right. You can't let off passengers up this way."

"I don't intend to," I said.

He glanced at Katharine, who was once again in the back seat. "You picked a passenger *up* here?" Clearly, if I'd done so, it had been in a somehow illegal manner.

I said, "No, I didn't pick her up here."

"Brother," he said, "you got to be doing one or the other, either bringing a passenger here or taking a passenger away from here."

Katharine, leaning forward, said, "Tom? What's the matter?"

"Just a misunderstanding." To the cop, I said, "I'm not actually a cab, not the way you think I am."

"You sure *look* like a cab."

"Well, I am. But I'm a New York City cab."

He beetled his brows at me, then got a little smug smirk on his face and said, "Oh, yeah? Myself, I happen to be from the planet Mars."

"Really? Is it true those aren't actually canals?"

"All right, smart guy, pull off on the grass."

I said, "You wouldn't happen to have noticed my license plate, would you?"

No, he wouldn't have. Beginning to wonder just who was kidding who around here, he backed away, frowning massively at me through the windshield until he reached the front of the cab, when he transferred his frown to my license plate. His lips moved. He brooded at the plate. He looked at me some more, through the windshield. He came back to the window and said, "Okay, fella. And just what in holy hell are you doing *here*?"

"Passing through."

"Then keep passing," he said, with a jerking motion of his thumb. "And don't let me see you here again."

What is it that makes cops so insecure? "I won't," I assured him, and drove on.

"Tom?"

"It was just a mistake," I said, not bothering to look in the mirror.

"Not that," she said. "This may surprise you, since it isn't even three o'clock, but what I was thinking of was lunch."

"Oh, lunch. Right, lunch." What with my hangover, and my larger-than-normal breakfast, and the rush to get to Kansas City on time, and the activities since, I'd completely forgotten about lunch, but now that she'd mentioned it I did notice a kind of vacant feeling around my middle. "I'll stop as soon as I see a place," I promised.

"Fine."

There was a diner near the airport. I pointed to it, calling, "Look okay to you?"

Katharine said, "Will they give me food if I cry and beg and scream?"

"Okay," I said, and pulled in there, and we took a table at a window overlooking the cab. I might almost have been in the Market Diner on Eleventh Avenue, except for the different brand of English being spoken: R's were being pronounced all over the place, but on the other hand the G of ING was being left silent. Also, the waitress smiled when she took our order; chef salad and iced coffee for Katharine, the shrimp salad platter and iced tea for me. Then I sat looking at my cab until Katharine said, "I wish you'd tell me about it."

I shook my head at her. "I really don't have anything to tell. Just a bad mood, that's all. Probably the hangover."

"Something happened while we were in that conference room," she insisted. "Everything was all right when we went in there, but all of a sudden at the end you were in a bad mood."

Shrugging, I said, "It's over now, or it's going away. Does it matter?"

"Yes. I thought we were becoming friends. I thought I could talk with you."

"You can," I said irritably. "Listen, everybody has moods, right? So I had a mood, and now I don't have it anymore."

"What did I do wrong?" she asked me. "What upset you?"

"You didn't do anything wrong. How do I know what you did wrong; I'm no landscape architect."

She frowned at me, thinking it over. The waitress brought our iced tea and coffee, and I busied myself with stirring. You put sugar in iced tea, it means a lot of stirring.

Katharine said, musingly, "It isn't as simple as that, it isn't just male envy about me having a good job. You're not like that, or it would have shown up before."

"Look, Katharine," I said, "it wasn't anything at all. Let it drop, okay?"

"No. It *was* something. Please, Tom, I just want to understand. What bothered you in there?"

*Clink-clink-clink-clink-clink.* I watched the long spoon in the iced tea, with the insoluble sugar grains whirling around and around and around. Nobody spoke. I sneaked a look up through my eyebrows, and Katharine was watching me. *Clink-clink-clink-clink-clink.* I sighed, shook my head, stopped stirring, put both palms on the tabletop, looked over to see if maybe the waitress would rescue me by bringing the food, sighed again and said, while watching another waitress behind the main counter slice a pie, "How come he didn't sit down?"

"Sit down?" Bewilderment in the tone; I still wasn't looking at her. "You mean Roy?"

"It wasn't a master–servant thing," I said. "I mean, you hired me too, and I was sitting down. We're eating lunch together, at the same table."

"I've never thought about it," she said, sounding honestly surprised; when I flashed her a quick glance, I could see she wasn't offended but interested. She said, "It's just the normal way, with a secretarial assistant. If you're giving dictation, the secretary sits on the other side of the desk, but— Oh, I see, of course. If you're just going over papers together, normal instructions, things like that, it's necessary for the secretary or messenger or whoever to be on the same side of the desk, so, they can see the papers, understand what's going on. But it would be cumbersome to have a second chair back there."

"You weren't at a desk. You were at a conference table."

"Habit," she said. "It didn't occur to me to ask Roy to sit, and I'm sure it didn't occur to him."

"I see what you mean," I said. "Okay. Sure."

She gave me a keen look. "But that wasn't the whole point," she said. "There's still something stuck in your craw."

"Well, it isn't lunch," I said, looking away toward the counter. "Where *is* that girl?"

"It's the male–female thing," Katharine insisted. "Otherwise, it wouldn't bother you this way. You're very straightforward about things, but now you're just ducking and hiding."

"Am I?" I looked at her straight, and tried to think about it. "It just bothered me. I think it was more age than sex. I mean, if he'd been some kid straight out of college it wouldn't have been anything at all."

"His age? What difference does it make what age he is? He's not exactly doddering."

"He's not exactly a world-beater either," I said. "The guy's maybe fifty, the suit's a little seedy…" I shrugged, not knowing how to express it.

"You've spent the last two days," Katharine said, "giving me your philosophy about consciously *not* being a world-beater. What is this sudden change?"

"I felt sorry for the guy. My philosophy isn't necessarily his philosophy. I mean, look at the suit; he's still trying to put on that façade, right? And he's missed the boat, he's *never* going to make it, and he's having his nose rubbed in it."

"His nose rubbed in it? How?"

"Standing there, having some—"

Silence. Bright-eyed, Katharine watched me. She wouldn't even *ask* me to finish the sentence, damn her.

Now that it was too late, the cavalry arrived, with the chef salad and the shrimp salad platter. Neither of us noticed her putting the plates in the wrong places; after she left, I looked down—for something to do with my eyes—and found myself staring at chef salad. "She mixed them up," I said, and made something of a production out of switching them. Then I looked up again, and Katharine was still watching me. "Okay," I said.

"Some—"

I nodded. "You're right. Thank you; I didn't know that was in there. Here's this guy, old enough to be my father, all of his failed hopes and ambitions written all over his suit and his face and the way he combs his hair, and it seems like a worse indignity than usual that he has to be bossed around by some woman half his age. That's right, that's what I thought. Let the bastard sit down and you'll be like equals and I won't mind it, I won't feel sorry for him anymore."

"If I were a man," she asked, "and he was still the same person, and still standing there?"

"If you were a man *his age*, then it's the fall of the dice. Men are in competition with one another. Peers are in competition with one another. Here's a winner, there's a loser, that's okay, it's the way of the world. If on the other hand you were a man *your* age, and Roy's boss, I'd start to feel sorry for the guy. With you a woman, I feel more sorry."

"And if I were a woman his age?"

I thought about it. "Slight pity, very slight. But the generation thing, that's important. The rules have changed in the last generation. If that guy is secretary to a woman his own age, they were all operating under the same rules, and she had to work damn hard to be where she is instead of where he is. But the new women coming along have it easier, they don't have to work anywhere near as hard."

"Not much harder than men, in fact," Katharine said, with a small smile.

"Exactly. And whatever people say on the surface, there's this underground feeling that there's something *unfair* about it."

"Unfair about equality?"

"That's right. The rules used to be, it's tougher for women. So if a man finds a woman above him, he knows she really *has* to be better than he is, and he doesn't have to worry about it. But now he can look at a woman, she's in the first place a woman, and in the second place younger than him, and she's his boss, and she didn't have to try *any* harder. Because the root idea is, women aren't *supposed* to have ambitions or a need for success, except the exceptional few, and they don't count. But now there's women all over the place. You're maybe the generation that gained the equality, but Roy's the generation that lost the privileges." With an attempt at an ironic smile, I said, "Male supremacy, the double standard, all that stuff, there were *some* people they were good for."

"Not really," she said. "Studies show that men aren't truly happy in that relationship with women."

"Studies also can be full of shit. You can do all the reading you want in the eighteenth and nineteenth centuries, you'll find men complaining about this and that and the other, but you won't find them objecting to their male prerogatives."

"They didn't understand the problem." Then she shook her head and said, "And you aren't any nineteenth century man, or at least you haven't been. Or is this the real you coming out?"

"Maybe," I said. "What I was feeling about Roy—and if you stop and think about it I don't actually have that much sense of kinship with Roy—but what I was feeling wasn't the result of a thought-out approach to life. It came out of irrational prejudices I wasn't even thinking about. So you started pulling on the end of the string, and this is what's emerging."

"And what do you think of it all?"

"I think it's silly. If we're talking about rational thought, I *think* Roy's life has nothing to do with your life. His existence has nothing to do with whether you're good at your job. I'm a little surprised to see I had this stuff inside me, and all I can say is, it was left over."

She suddenly laughed; more from relief, I think, than anything else. "You were arguing so *forcefully*," she said, "I really thought you meant it all."

"Well, of course I mean it all, only I didn't know it. If you'd asked me about the subject ahead of time, given me some hypothetical example, I would have answered you from the rational top of my head and thought I was telling the truth."

"And now?"

I shrugged. "We always have a few surprises left for ourselves. Considering my marriage, considering my relationships with women the last few years, it's very likely I have a few surprises more tucked away inside my head."

"Like me, with Barry."

I gave her a sharp look. "Meaning what?"

"Well, I suppose some male–female thing down in my subconscious could be what's giving me trouble," she said. "Keeping me from total commitment."

"Such as what?"

But she laughed again, and shook her head. "It isn't that easy, Tom. You got surprised into it."

"Some time between here and Los Angeles," I promised, "I'll sneak up behind you and say *Boo*."

"Good," she said. "But in the meantime, may we *please* eat?"

So we ate.

## 21

Kansas. Now I know what flat is.

Of course, that was just as well, because we had to make up lost time. When we left the diner after our late lunch it was nearly four o'clock, and we'd so far done less than two hundred miles on the day. I was determined to reach five hundred before we quit, so it was a good thing most of the road in front of us would be straight and flat. Which it was; I seemed to be driving across a dining room table not yet set for dinner. I kept feeling like Gulliver in Brobdingnag, and I wouldn't have been at all surprised if a giant hand had all at once reached down out of the sky, picked us up cab and all, and moved us to another part of the gameboard.

Katharine and I were friends once more. She sat up front, and our conversation was all inconsequential; past vacation experiences, college days, the lack of variety in the world around us. Her relief was so great at not having to make the Great Decision today after all that I doubt she gave Barry more than a passing thought for the rest of the afternoon; I know she didn't mention him. Between our idle chit-chats I at times brooded on our conversation in the diner, making some small effort to understand myself but not much getting anywhere.

Reversing our sidetrip to the airport initially meant dropping south on Interstate 635, taking a toll bridge across the Missouri River, and playing bumper-cars with the beginnings of rush-hour traffic down Route 70, which here had become the Kansas Turnpike; a toll road. Between Kansas City, where we got on, and Topeka, where we got off fifty miles later, it cost us just over a dollar.

Topeka is considerably smaller than Kansas City, but by now it was also considerably closer to five o'clock, and even though it was Saturday, traffic was as clogged as a nose in hay-fever time. Frustration was beginning to get to me; even though one of the first things you learn as a cabdriver is that in most situations—careless pedestrians excepted—your horn is absolutely useless, I actually found myself, on Route 70 in mid-Topeka, while ambling along beside the equally slow (but opposite-directioned) Kansas River, leaning on my horn.

With Topeka at last behind us, we could begin to make some time, troubled now only by the ever-present threat of Highway Patrols and that huge gold sun gradually setting just past the tip of my nose. The road was dull and flat and straight, the traffic finally thinning, the sun so glaring it was impossible to see anything, the afternoon air dry and hot, and I slowly thickened into an automaton role; the robot at the wheel. It's the worst kind of driving, really, the most endlessly monotonous and therefore eventually dangerous. Katharine napped, the orange sun giving her smooth face a veneer of stage makeup, and I told myself stories, counted red cars, brooded about my sexist tendencies, and even turned on the radio a while. I could get no commercial stations, of course, but I did listen to the pilot's half of a conversation with the control tower at something apparently called Philip Billard Airport; I can't begin to guess where that might be. Switching from channel to channel I picked up other stray fragments of conversation, but never enough to make sense of it.

*Dreary* driving. The sun just hung there, dead ahead, getting bigger and refusing to sink. I did seventy-five, I did eighty, I even crept to eighty-five once or twice though the cab didn't like it, and with that sun in my eyes neither did I. Katharine awoke and was logy and cranky, not wanting to talk, not finding it possible to get comfortable in the front seat with both the meter and my license-mount in her knee-space. Perspiration pearled her upper lip and made her hair dank around her ears. "I can't *stand* this," she said, and climbed over to the back seat. In the mirror I could see her trying to go back to sleep and failing. Then she sat up and morosely watched the roadside; she looked very sorry to be here. As were we all.

Miles and miles and miles. Paxico, Manhattan (one of God's bad jokes), Junction City, Moonlight (now *there's* a town name), Abilene, Selina, Lincoln, Black Wolf, Dorrance, Bunker Hill (they're kidding), Homer, Victoria, Catharine. "There's your town," I said.

"They spelled it wrong." So much for high spirits.

The bottom of the sun trembled above the horizon but wouldn't touch it. My ribs were sore, my right knee was sore. My cheeks ached from squinting so long. The gas station and motel signs thrust high in the air on their stalk legs at every exit were only black silhouettes in the orange glare, their cleverly plotted colors and lettering and designs all obliterated by that infernal sun.

We were approaching an exit. From the back seat the cranky voice came: "It's after eight o'clock."

I looked at the speedometer; less than four hundred fifty miles on the day. "We got a late start," I said. "I'm trying to make up lost time."

"Tom," she said, and her voice trembled, "we have to get *out* of this car."

"Right," I said, and swerved, took the exit.

# 22

It was the same room. The exit we'd taken from Route 70 had come equipped with a Holiday Inn, and my room was the same one I'd already been given twice. Except I think the non-Utrillos were reversed; wasn't the one with the sleeping laundry pile on the left last night?

The world was hot and dry, while Katharine and I were hot and muggy. She made the booking arrangements alone again tonight and we went to our rooms with a minimum of conversation, not even making plans for dinner. My room was farther along the hall from hers, and in it the air-conditioning was on but not doing much. I turned it to a more Arctic setting, pulled open the drapes, and found myself facing that monstrous sun. It *still* hadn't set. Feeling a morbid fascination on the subject— was this the day the Earth stood still?—I left the drapes open, stripped off most of my clothing, and dropped myself like a piece of lumber onto the bed, where at last I began to read about the family Gritbone.

When the sun finally did go down, hundreds and hundreds of miles to the west across this flat landscape, it went all of a sudden, as though abruptly realizing how late it was. I left the Gritbone farm—drought, at the moment—long enough to watch the sun's exit, then with all the western sky a fiery red I closed the drapes and went on reading for another half hour or so, until the phone rang.

By now I'd recovered enough to be civil. "Hello. Katharine?"

"Hi, Tom, how are you?" She too had recovered.

"Semi-human. And you?"

"Was I awful in the car?"

"The *world* was awful. You put up with it very well."

"At one point there I was ready to start biting things."

"If you'll look at the steering wheel, you see toothmarks."

She laughed, and said, "On a similar topic, I just called the restaurant, and they only serve till ten o'clock."

"On a Saturday night?"

"That's what they said."

"I am a stranger in a strange land. What time is it now?" My watch, as usual, was in the cab.

"Just after nine-thirty."

"In other words, we ought to go do it."

"If we want dinner."

"I'll call for you in fifteen minutes," I said, and did, and we headed for the restaurant.

It's always possible, in these sprawled-out motels, to travel from place to place inside them via endless anonymous narrow corridors, but if the weather's at all acceptable one tends to go outside and circle the building to one's destination. That's what we did this time, going past our by-now very dusty and scruffy cab, and finding the sky a mad psychedelic array of color; purples, mauves, indigos, navy blues, violets, amethysts, garnets, vermilions, all were streaked and swathed and swept across that huge curved canvas as though God had never heard that less is more. All afternoon an incomprehensible feeling had been coming over me, while driving into that glaring golden sun, and now I understood: "We're on a different planet."

Katharine said, "Is that what it is? I knew there was something; I felt that time had stopped. Did you ever read Ray Bradbury?"

"Sure." Then I frowned at her. "Girls don't read science fiction."

"There you go again," she said.

We went on to the restaurant, where the headwaiter, though

male, adapted readily to Katharine's being host. He looked to be a college student with a part-time job, but he was bright and alert and efficient, and after he'd taken our drink orders and departed I said, "Looks as though you won't save much on the tip tonight."

"It has its compensations. I once *wrote* a science fiction story."

"Oh, come on."

"It's true," she said. "In college. Would you like to hear it?"

"Of course."

She said, "It was about the Solar System going through a mysterious space cloud, and afterwards the atmosphere on Earth is changed. There's this new element in it that the scientists don't understand, but it reacts with women's bodies so that if a woman wants to get pregnant all she has to do is eat honey. I called it 'You're My Honey.' Now, the thing is, this makes it possible for women to have children without the assistance of men, but the children are all girls. Male children only result from the traditional method. So it's up to women whether or not they want men in the world anymore, since men aren't necessary for reproducing the human race but only for reproducing men."

"Hmmmm," I said.

"I was very militant then," she said.

"So it was decided to do without men?"

"Just listen," she said, as our drinks arrived. She waited till the waitress had served them, and distributed menus, and then she continued: "At first, the men don't take it seriously, but then the statistics show a higher and higher percentage of female births, and around the world different governments set up commissions to see what's going on. But of course the commissions are all men, except for a token woman here and there, like in the United States and Great Britain, so they have no idea what's going on, and they don't get anywhere. Then the men counterattack. The incidence of rape goes up, as men try to make women pregnant before they can make themselves pregnant. Some countries like Russia outlaw honey and try to wipe out the world's population of bees, but bees are very hard to get rid of entirely, and very easy to breed surreptitiously, so there's an ongoing black market in honey."

"This is a hell of a story."

She smiled at me, a bit smugly. "The boy I was going with at the time couldn't stand it. He kept saying it showed I hated him personally."

"Instead of men in general."

"Well, that too," she admitted. "But I think the way Danny described it, I was *afraid* of men in general, but I *hated* him in particular."

"Was this the Tupperware fellow?"

"No, before him."

"Go on with the story," I said. "As a man, you might say I'm dying to find out how it ends."

But the waitress was beside us, and Katharine said, "I think we ought to order."

The waitress, looking apologetic, said, "I don't want to rush you, but the kitchen's about to close."

"Half the human race hangs in the balance," I said, "and *she's* worried about the kitchen. All right, all right." And I did a quick scan of the menu.

Restaurant menus, away from the major cities, don't vary that much. There's six or seven things you recognize, time after time, and you just order one of them, because you know they know how to make it and they know you know what it should taste like. So we placed our dinner orders without too much difficulty, and then I took a quick swallow of my gin and tonic and said, "On with the story. At this point, the male population is killing bees and raping women, while the female population is smuggling honey and having daughters."

Laughing, she said, "Well, of course, not everybody reacts the same way. There are loving married couples who go on as before, and there are men who try to come to an understanding of the situation, and there are women who try to work out what best to do. And a leader of the moderate women, from the group that believes each individual should follow her own conscience, is elected President of the United States. Naturally."

"Naturally?"

"Well, there are more women than men, and the disparity is growing every day. As for it being a moderate woman, American voters always tend toward the center. When it becomes clear that women have the final *control* in the solution of the problem, the men in both major parties put women candidates up for President, and of course one of them wins."

"Okay," I said.

"With the American government leading the way," she continued, "power around the globe gradually shifts from the men to the women. Women take over industry, commerce, everything, and always using the same ultimate threat: 'If men make us angry, there won't *be* any more men.'"

"I rate this story very high for suspense," I said.

"Well, finally there's a mass meeting. A global meeting, with the American Congress and the UN and the British Parliament and the Japanese Diet and all the other legislatures—and by now they're all almost completely women—all connected together by TV. And there's a great debate about the future of mankind. Because by now a lot of women want to ban male births completely, with jail sentences for the mother and—if they can find him—the father. In seventy or eighty years, if they have their way, there won't be any more men at all, anywhere, and there never will be a man again because it takes a man to make a male child."

She sipped at her drink, then went on: "And the debate ends with a speech from the American president, who first talks about all the trouble that men have been to women down the ages, oppressing women, enslaving women, making women the villains in all their religions and superstitions. And then all the trouble men have been to one another and to all the other creatures on this planet. And *then* she says, 'The reason they've been so much trouble to everybody is because *they* always had to decide. Whether it was hunting a mammoth for food for the family or competing for a better job so they could move the kids to the suburbs, it has almost always been the man who had the responsibility, and too much responsibility makes anybody nervous and erratic. Now *we* have the responsibility, and those who say we should do away with men are themselves being nervous and erratic. We have one great advantage, in that we can profit by their mistakes. We *can* be calm. We have the power, and we can't possibly lose it. So we can stop looking at men out of bitterness and grievance, and we can see they have some good qualities as well. They're very good at building things. Some of them are fairly useful at fixing things. They have an eagerness for life which has helped them deal with too much responsibility, and which in repose can be rather lovable. They are capable of being excellent companions, and to be practical there is no acceptable substitute in bed. The best man is not, as some have suggested, a dead man, but a retired man, all responsibility finished. A putterer, a permanent boy. It will take men a while to adapt themselves to this new role, but women adapted themselves to subservience for thousands of years and men, too, will find it possible to adjust. So long as there are women, there *must* go on being men, to be our companions, our help-mates, our better halves, our assistants and auxiliaries. In a word, our wives!'"

Having finished this speech with every evidence of relish, Katharine smiled a great beaming smile and drained her drink. Simultaneously our appetizers arrived, and I looked at mine with little appetite. I said, "That's some story."

"What do you think of it?"

"Was it published?"

"In 1968?" With a sardonic grin, she shook her head.

"I think it's—got a certain amount of hostility in it," I said.

"You don't think it ends on a positive note?"

Then I realized she was laughing at me. "A very positive note," I acknowledged. "After all, early retirement is the primary tenet of my whole approach to life."

Overtly laughing, she said, "You *are* my post-revolution man, aren't you?"

"Maybe. Are you still that hostile? Seriously, if you are it could say a lot about your problems in re Barry."

"No, I don't think so," she said, more somberly. "I went through college just at the beginning of the women's move-ment, and my consciousness was raised just in time to see the incredible difference in reasonable expectation between me and the boys I knew, a *lot* of whom were very much dumber than me."

"We're opposites," I said. "Too much was expected from me, so I stopped pushing. Too little was expected from you, so you started pushing."

"That's rather glib," she suggested.

"But it makes an interesting point, maybe. And you know what they say about opposites."

"Birds of a feather flock together?"

"Not exactly. Shall we eat our appetizers?"

We ate for a while, during which I pondered Katharine's story. Between the appetizer and the entrée I said, "You know, with so much bad history and grievances between the sexes, it's amazing any couples ever get together at all."

"*Getting* together is easy," she said. "Biology takes care of that. It's the staying together that's tough. A couple begins in love and happiness, and then they spiral down through bad experiences and misunderstandings and mutual cruelties until they either split or they find an accommodation in which they live together without having anything to do with one another. Everybody I know is on that spiral. That's one of the things that bothers me when I think about Barry. I do love Barry, Tom, I really do. I love him too much to get on that spiral with him. But is there any other way?"

"There must be happy couples around," I said.

"Name six."

"Maybe it's just a phase this society is going through. Didn't there *used* to be happy couples?"

"Because the divorce rate was lower? Divorce was less acceptable then, that's all. Catholic couples today don't divorce; are all Catholic marriages happy?"

"You're extremely negative," I said.

"You should talk. The first time I mentioned marriage to you, you made a face."

"Because it wasn't any good for *me*. But it's got to be good for some people. Like my parents." Then I thought about my parents and said, "No, cancel that. My parents are happy, but not with each other. They can't count as a couple."

"Marriage is a serious step," Katharine said.

"Just like those pamphlets in the back of the church used to say."

Smiling, she said, "I think everybody, before they get married, should take a cab across the country and think it over."

"There's already too much traffic. Let them take bicycles to Asbury Park."

On that note we left it, because the wine arrived, immediately followed by the main course. The discussion didn't pick up again until we'd finished the food and were on the last of the wine, when Katharine said, "As a matter of fact, I'm *not* that hostile anymore. That was a very youthful thing, and full of brand new shock and outrage."

"It's a strong story," I said. "If it was told well, it could be very effective."

"When *Ms.* magazine came along, I thought of rewriting it and sending it there. That was after the Reich book, so I was going to change the honey to green beans and call it 'The Green Beaning of America.' "

"That's awful."

"True. Anyway, I got the story out and looked at it again, and I just didn't feel that way anymore. Or at least not enough to retype the whole story. Also, the writing wasn't very good. Besides, by then I knew I really liked men. I like men who don't feel they have to stand on top of me in order to be tall. Such as Barry. Or you."

"Thank you."

"I do like you, Tom," she said, and either it was the lighting or the wine but her face seemed softer, the bone structure less obvious. She was beautiful under all circumstances.

"It's mutual," was all I felt secure enough to say.

Katharine signaled for the check, signed it, and we left. The sky now was diamonds on black velvet, with a great gibbous moon rising from the direction of New York. The moon looked like a polished semi-circular piece of milk glass, with a powerful light shining through it. The parked cars we walked past were hulked sleeping beasts, moonlight glittering from the chrome of their fenders and swimming in the depths of their windows. We stopped near the cab, by mutual consent, and stood gazing up at the sky. Then I looked at her raised profile, and put my hand on her shoulder: "Katharine."

Gently but immediately she slid away from the hand. "We already talked about that, Tom."

"In the abstract. What you're looking at now is concrete."

"Tom, don't confuse the issue."

"Why should the issue be better off than I am?"

"Tom—" She hesitated, frowning at me in a troubled way, then glanced around as if for help, then frowned at me once more. Gently, sympathetically, she said, "Tom. Read your cab." And she turned and walked quickly away toward the stairs.

Read my cab? Of course that was just a distraction, to keep me from following her at once, but what had she meant? The cab was clearly visible in the gray-white moonlight; from here I could see the rear deck and part of the left side. I could just barely make out the rates posted on the outside of the driver's door. Stenciled on the passenger's door was my father's company name: "Harflet Livery Service Co." On the trunk lid were several items: the large decal from Speediphone Cab, giving the company name and phone number; the decal from LOMTO, the League of Metered Taxicab Owners; the black number 27, being this cab's call-number with Speediphone; and—

Oh.

Spread across the trunk lid, in firm black letters, was the standard notice to tailgaters:

"Keep Your Distance."

## 23

In my dream the women decided to get rid of all the men except me. A delegation, led by Anne Bancroft, came to the room in which I was being kept and said to me, "All the other men are being put to death, but we're keeping you around in case any women want to have sons." I said, "Why me?" They said, "Isn't that what men want, to have all the women on Earth? You'll be the only man, and any woman who wants a son will have to go to bed with you. You'll have thousands of women." And I said, "But I don't want thousands of women. All I want is Katharine."

I count it as a nightmare.

# 24

I was prepared next morning to apologize for the night before, and to promise I'd do no more tailgating, but Katharine chose to behave as though nothing had happened and I was delighted to go along. We had an early breakfast and drove briskly out onto Route 70, the now-tame sun a beneficent smiling face in the sky behind us. Katharine rode up front and we played word games: Superghost and Twenty Questions. An hour and a half later we lost an hour, zipping across an invisible line from Central to Mountain Time.

Kansas continued flat, but the weather became less certain. Far to the north we could see small rainstorms sweeping across the land like black-sailed ships from the Spanish Armada. From time to time a cloud glided across the beaming sun-face, and some of the traffic coming from the opposite direction had its headlights on, but the storms never quite reached us.

Kansas became Colorado at a town unhappily called Kanorado. This is a fairly common thing for state-line towns to do, cobble up a name from both state names, and the result is rarely euphonious to either the ear or the eye. There's Mexhoma and Texhoma and Texico; Laark and Arkana and Texarkana; Florala, Monida, and Virgilina; Tennemo and Arkoma and Uvada; Marydel *and* Delmar. Mexicali and Calexico are across the border from one another. The towns that simply call themselves State Line are a lot better off.

The change of state occurred without much change of landscape, and travel ennui began to set in; we gave up both games and conversation, and drove in a bored patient silence for half an hour or so, until Katharine suddenly sat up and said, "Hey! I did this road!"

"You what?"

"This is *my* road," she said, and when I frowned at her in bewilderment she was staring out at the highway with every sign of pleasure and excitement. "Yes," she said, as though some long-held theory of hers was being vindicated, "yes, yes…"

"You mean— Wait a minute. You mean you *landscaped* this?"

"That's right. Those shrubs— That's exactly what I thought; give it two or three years— There should be a hill along here, on the right, I put it in. Yes, there it is. See it?"

Ahead of us, on the right, was a low hill covered with young trees. I said, "You mean that was flat before? You *put* that hill there?"

"There's some sort of meat-packing plant off that way," she said. "The ugliest thing you ever saw. So we hid it."

"You put in a hill." I couldn't believe it. In my head, a landscape architect hadn't been anything more than a person who comes in with a lot of seeds and maybe some rose bushes. But this was something else again; to change the face of the land, to put in your own hill, to force trees and ground and shrubbery to conform to aesthetic decisions—I stared out at Katharine's road in astonishment verging on awe.

And Katharine continued to comment on the results of her labors. "That's *perfect*," she said. "Oh, yes, that's filling in so well. Those shrubs in the central mall; they cut down headlight glare at night *and* they make a good flexible barrier to contain a car that's gone out of control, but at the same time they don't get in the way of the view."

What a strange feeling, to drive along on a person's work of art. There was practically no other traffic, and we in the cab seemed to float through Katharine's landscape as though our wheels were two feet above the ground. We soared along in bright sunlight, gazing left and right like children's-story characters in a magic flying shoe arriving at the fairy kingdom. "We did eight miles of it," Katharine said, her voice hushed as though a loud sound might break the spell.

The most incredible eight miles. Katharine pointed out this and that item, told me why this had been done, what had been changed over there, what the theories were behind the various decisions, and I found I was alternately grinning at the highway and grinning at Katharine. "Fantastic," I kept saying. It was like having a painter invite you *into* his latest painting for a little walk around and a guided tour.

"And that's it," she said at last, and craned around to look back.

"Why did it stop after eight miles?"

"It was a pilot project, with Federal financing. They're doing a number of studies around the country, and eventually they may put up funds for a lot more. Usually, you know, when they build these highways, they just grade with a bulldozer and let it go at that."

"Well," I said, "I think the Federal government ought to hire you to do every road in the country."

Katharine laughed, very pleased, and for the next fifteen minutes or so we talked about her work. At one point I said, "There's a funny kind of link between you and Barry, isn't there? What he does with faces you do with the land."

"We've noticed that," Katharine told me. "We decided one time we'd go into business together after we got married, offer to do people's noses and lawns all at once, for a blanket price."

"You and Barry get along, don't you?" I was annoyed to see that the idea troubled me.

"Of course we do," she said. "That's why he wants to marry me, and why I *think* I want to marry him. When you two finally meet, in Los Angeles, you'll like him."

"Okay," I said. And when I glanced over at her, she was giving me a knowing smirk.

# 25

Sooner or later, when you're traveling, you have to think about laundry. Katharine and I were driving along, discussing the idea of doing our accumulated laundry today during our lunch-stop if we could find a laundromat open on Sunday, when all at once she frowned past me and said, "That fellow's signaling at you."

"Fellow?" Looking to my left, I saw a blue Mercury in the next lane, with a cheery round-faced thirtyish man grinning and waving at me. Another case of astonishment at a New York City cab way out here, etc? I smiled and waved back, but that wasn't enough for him; grinning, he pointed at his ears, then held something up, then pantomimed speaking into his hand.

No; into his microphone. That's what it was, a microphone he was alternately waving and speaking into. Intrigued despite myself, I switched on my radio and went from channel to channel until all at once a voice heavy with static spoke loudly, saying, "—ears on?"

Was that him? Glancing in his direction, I held up one finger. He nodded and grinned and spoke. The voice on the radio said, "One." I held up two fingers, and the voice said, "Two." Then it said, "Well, good buddy, now you've got your ears on."

My ears on? The CB craze had swept the nation without catching me in its toils—if you spend ten hours every day with Hilda the Dispatcher snarling at you from a radio next to your knee you don't particularly need a lot *more* radio in your life—but I did know enough to recognize that the sentence, "Well, good buddy, now you've got your ears on," meant, "Hello, friend, you're receiving my signal." So I unlimbered my own microphone and said, "Yes, I've got you."

"Ten-one, good buddy," said the voice. "Give us more volume." Simultaneously, he was dropping back, pulling into my lane behind me.

"Okay," I said, speaking more loudly. "How's this?"

"Ten-four. And hello to the seatcover."

I frowned at the Mercury now in my rearview mirror. "Beg pardon?"

"The beaver," he said.

I hadn't the vaguest idea what he was talking about. "Oh," I said. "Sure."

"Nice to eyeball you," he said. "I'm Screaming Eagle. What's *your* handle?"

Handle; nickname. "Umm, the Yellow Cabby," I said.

"You're from the dirty side, huh?"

Was I? It's true the cab wasn't the cleanest vehicle on the road, but was that a fit topic for conversation? "I guess so," I said.

"Where you headed?"

"California."

"Shaky side," he commented.

"If you say so."

"Ten-nine?"

That was a question, obviously, but what question was it? "I'm not sure I follow you," I said.

"We've got a ten-one, good buddy. We may have to back out."

"Well, you'd know best." Ahead was an exit; we'd been planning to stop for lunch soon anyway, and I was more than ready to say goodbye to my new friend. "This is our exit," I told him.

"Ten-four, good buddy. All the good numbers."

"Uh huh."

I was slowing for the exit. This madman passed me, waving still with his cheery smile. His voice came one last time from the radio: "Don't feed the bears."

"Oh, I won't," I promised, and rolled around the curving exit ramp.

Katharine said, "What was *that* all about?"

"You know just as much as I do." Putting my mike back on its hook, I stopped at the red blinker and studied the sign across the way, giving town names and directions and distances. The nearest town was apparently one mile to the left, so that's the way I turned.

Katharine said, "That was fascinating. Do you mind if I fool with the radio? Maybe we could pick up some more conversations."

"You *liked* that conversation? Go ahead."

"Well, maybe we'll find somebody who speaks English."

I drove on into town while Katharine fiddled with the radio. I wanted a laundromat first, so I turned where a sign pointed to 'Town Center,' finding myself on a curving blacktop road in a well-to-do residential neighborhood; large new houses with attached garages set well back from the road on both sides. Katharine was picking up static, stray bits of broadcasting voices, but nothing particularly coherent or interesting. We drove along, rather slowly, and then I became aware of something odd happening in my rearview mirror. I peered more closely, then double-checked in my outside mirror, and said, "Omigosh. Katharine, turn it off."

"Why? What's the matter?"

"Look behind us."

She did. "Are *we* doing that?"

"The radio," I said.

Down the road behind us, every remote-control garage door was going crazy: o-pen-and-close-and-o-pen-and-close-and-o-pen-and-close-and—

"Turn it off, Katharine!"

"I don't know how! Which switch?"

So I turned it off myself, then looked back to see all those garage doors finishing whichever part of the cycle they'd been on. At last they all stopped, but not exactly as before; some that had been closed were now open, and some that had been open were now closed. And from the houses baffled people were emerging, looking at their garages and at one another and at the sky.

Katharine was laughing. I said, "Don't laugh, this is serious. We may have started a new religion."

## 26

There was not only a laundromat open on Sunday, it was full. We waited five minutes or so until two machines became free, then loaded them up; whites in this one, colored in that one. There's a strange comic intimacy when your laundry shares a washing machine with her laundry; 'comic' because you can't make the slightest reference to it without feeling like a fool.

While our laundry soaked and swirled, we had lunch in an Ice Cream Parlor, an absolutely straightforward honest-to-God Ice Cream Parlor, complete with the marble counter and the booths with the tall dark-wood seatbacks and the slow-moving ceiling fans. And not some tarted-up imitation, full of fake nostalgia and tacky with-itness, named something like Banana Splitsville; this was Thrughauser's Ice Cream Parlor, and it was the real thing. At two booths in the back some 1947 teenagers were discussing cars, dates and high school. The old gent behind the counter was everybody's gray-moustached uncle. And the lady in the black dress and white apron who took our orders was stout, motherly, and cheerful.

Great hamburgers, with relish. Great coffee. And ice cream for dessert, also great. "Maybe we can buy a house and stay forever," I said.

"What *I'm* afraid of," Katharine said, "is we'll still be here when the town sinks beneath the surface, and you know it won't rise again for a hundred years."

"There are worse fates."

Back at the laundromat, our wash was ready for the dryer. We cajoled the machine with many dimes, then went away to feed gas to the cab. What we found was a gas station with a connecting car wash. "It's laundry day, right?" I said, and sent the cab through the car wash. Katharine got a road map from the gas station office, and stood in the sunshine perusing it. The cab came out the other end of the car wash gleaming and glistening, looking happier than I'd ever seen it. Taxicabs too need a vacation from the city.

One of the kids with the chamois cloths said to me, "Man, that's cool. You got this fixed up exactly like the real thing."

"I've even got a meter," I pointed out.

"I saw that. Terrific, man."

"Thanks."

Katharine and I got back into the cab, headed out to the street, and one of those clouds that had been walking around the sky all day paused directly overhead to dump eleven million gallons of rain on us. "God damn son of a bitch," I said. "I should have *known* better than get it washed."

We parked as close to the laundromat as we could get, and made a dash through the rain. The laundry wasn't dry yet—neither were we, anymore—so we sat to wait on two of the mismatched chrome tube chairs with which all laundromats are fitted out. Katharine still had the road map with her, and she said, "Tom, I've been thinking."

"Oh?"

"I don't know about you, but I'm getting sick of superhighways."

"*Your* little chunk wasn't so bad."

"But that was only eight miles, and there won't be any more of those." Opening the road map, she said, "Now, Route 70 angles way north from here, and goes up through Denver. But what if we took one of these other roads and just went straight west?"

"You're talking about the Rocky Mountains there."

"Well, these are still ordinary roads. It's not exactly like taking a Conestoga wagon into the wilderness."

"Also," I said, "it's raining."

"No, it isn't."

I turned to look out the window, and damn if the sun wasn't shining again.

"These will be perfectly fine roads," Katharine said. "They'll just be more real, that's all."

I too was sick of the Interstates, and was not at all eager to repeat yesterday afternoon's grinding experience of driving hour after hour directly into the sun, but on the other hand I knew this was simply another of Katharine's stalling techniques, and I thought the only honorable thing to do under the circumstances was be devil's advocate, so I said, "Katharine, you're just trying to delay things a little more."

"No, I'm not. This wouldn't be much longer at all. In the first place, Route 70 does this long loop around to the north, and we'd be going straight west, and a straight line is the shortest distance between two points."

"I've heard that someplace."

Ignoring my dumb levity, she said, "And in the second place, you know how the cities always slow us down, and Denver would be the same thing. If we take one of these roads—see them?—if we take one of them, we'll bypass all the big cities. Denver to the north, and Colorado Springs to the south. Then we'd connect up with Route 70 again somewhere on the other side." Putting the road map down, she said, "Come on, Tom, let's get *off* the highway for a while."

I was weakening. In fact, I was defeated, though I fought back feebly one last time: "Call Barry," I said. "Try the idea on him. If he says it's okay, then it's okay with me."

"Come on, Tom," she said. "You *know* I can get Barry to say yes."

"I just want you to go through the process."

"You just want to avoid the responsibility," she said accurately, and went away to twist Barry around her little finger.

## 27

The cab wouldn't start. Here we were with dry clothes on our bodies and clean clothes in our luggage, the rain replaced by wet shiny sunlight, the newly clean taxi gleaming like a Technicolor movie, and the damn thing refused to start. "*Grind, grind*," it said, and then, ominously, it said, "Click." It had never done that before. I released the key, then turned it again, and once again the starter said, "Click." I waited, holding the key in the ignition, but the starter had nothing else it wanted to say at this time.

Katharine, up front with me, frowned and said, "Something wrong?"

"Maybe not," I said, inanely. I manipulated the key twice more, being rewarded with one additional "click" each time, then finally gave it up and sat back to give the dashboard a look of dislike.

"What is it?"

"The starter," I said. "Or it could be something in the electrical system, but I think it's the starter. Here we are in Fat Chance, Colorado, on a Sunday, in a Checker cab, and we're going to need a new starter, or a new generator, or *some* damn new thing, and a mechanic to put it into the car, and I think we're in trouble."

"Oh, dear," she said.

"I'm sorry about this."

"It isn't *your* fault." She gazed forlornly out the windshield at what was essentially an alien land; that is to say, a typical American town. "Barry's going to be *so* upset."

"I'll talk to him," I offered.

She considered that, then slowly shook her head. "No, I don't think so."

"I'll have the mechanic talk to him. That is, if we find one. Let's see if there's a phonebook in the laundromat."

There was; a tiny thing, about the size of an expensive paperback edition of *Romeo and Juliet*, with a small round hole in the upper left corner through which a long dirty string tied it to a nail in the counter under the payphone on which Katharine had just extorted Barry's agreement to our change of route. In the yellow pages at the back of this book I found *Automobile Repairing & Svce*, phoned All Ready, Best Bros, Deep River Recking, Folonari, Kahn-Do, Kuhn's Kwality Svce, Motor Hotel, Pinetop Highway Garage and Smith's Svce, where at last a ringing phone was answered, by someone with a pleasant but gruff voice, saying, "*More* trouble."

"That's right," I said. "My car quit. I think it's the starter."

"Does it go *gruh-gruh-gruh*?" The sound he made was uncannily like a car when the battery is low.

"No," I said. "It goes *click*."

"Sounds like the starter," he admitted. "For openers, you're gonna need a tow."

"For starters," I punned. Or tried to.

"You'll need one a them, too, like as not. What make? Nothing foreign, I hope."

"Oh, no," I said. "One hundred percent American."

"Well," he said carefully, "nothing's one *hundred* percent American anymore. What are you driving, my friend?"

"Nothing at the moment. Until it stopped, a Checker."

Silence.

"Hello?"

"A Checker," came the subdued voice.

"It's American," I pointed out, rather defensively.

"So's Bigfoot," he said, rallying, "but I never seen one. Checker Marathon, eh?"

"Well, sort of."

"What do you mean, sort of?"

"Checker taxi, actually. It's about the same as a Marathon, a few alterations. Nothing under the hood, I think."

"One Bigfoot's about the same as another," he said. "Where is this creature?"

"Parked about two doors away from the Atomic Laundromat. I don't know what street, it's—"

"I know where it is. Yellow taxi?"

"That's right."

"Just like in the movies. Be there in ten minutes."

"Thanks," I said, and hung up, and stood frowning at the phone.

Katharine was watching my profile, and after a moment she said, "Well? What do you think?"

"I think," I said, "either he's going to be the most wonderful experience of our lives, or the worst disaster ever to befall a helpless New York City Checker taxicab."

# 28

The towtruck driver wasn't the same person I'd talked to on the phone, I knew that the instant I saw him, with his skinny body and his small oval head and his big mouth full of huge mismatched teeth. And it was confirmed an instant later when he spoke, in a high-pitched nasal voice, saying, "You the fella with the taxi?"

"That's right, Jerry," I said. He was wearing one of those dark green workshirts with your name in red script in a white oval on your left breast. His said *Jerry*.

Jerry pointed at the cab; the only yellow Checker taxicab in the state, probably, and certainly the only one in sight. "This it?"

"Sure is," I said. Was his partner going to be this smart? The fellow'd sounded sort of all right on the phone, but Jerry was increasing my sense of unease.

In any event, Jerry understood the workings of his own towtruck, and in less time than you could say "Jack Robinson" twice he'd hooked up, invited us into our cab for the journey, and we found ourselves sailing along through town with nothing in front of us but our own up-tilted hood; as though we were in some land-based variant of the motorboat.

"I've never traveled like this before," Katharine said, looking out cheerfully at the rain-fresh sidewalks, waving to children who giggled and waved back. "It's sort of fun."

"I have," I said. "And it's never been fun before. Of course, the other times it's always meant lost time and lost money."

"It's still lost time," she said, with a sunny smile.

"You're incorrigible," I told her.

Smith's Svce was a big sprawling concrete block building painted white and surrounded by blacktop. Gas pumps were in front, wheeled display racks filled with tires were to one side, and a lot of disreputable looking automobiles were parked here and there around the fringes. We stopped between the pumps and the building, Jerry yelled for us to get out, and out we climbed, down onto the blacktop, blinking in the sunlight and looking around.

While Jerry proceeded to back and fill and maneuver this way and that in order to run the Checker backwards through a big open garage door into the building, a small office door to the side opened and out came a burly-chested man with a thick black moustache and wearing a dark blue knit wool cap. This must be the man I'd spoken to on the phone, and the name in the oval on his workshirt was *Ralph*. Wanting to get on—or stay on—his good side, I approached with my hand out, saying, "Hi, Ralph, I'm Tom Fletcher, and this is—"

"Dave," he said, and took my hand, and shook it. "Pleased to meet you."

I stared at him. "What?"

"The name's Dave," he repeated. "Dave Smith. I'm the boss around here."

"Katharine Scott," Katharine said, smiling, and shook the man's hand.

I couldn't help it; I pointed at the name *Ralph* on that shirt. "But—" I said.

"Oh, this," he said, and chuckled down at the lie on his chest. "I'm a gambler," he explained. "They have these unclaimed freight sales every once in a while, you buy cartons contents unseen, you never know what you'll come up with. Paid three dollars, got two gross of these shirts here. All the names in the world. You're Tom, you say?"

"That's right."

"I got two Toms. You want 'em?"

"Thanks anyway," I said.

"No charge," he told me. "I got these shirts all over the place."

"I appreciate it," I said. "But—" And I fumbled, not knowing how to refuse the offer without seeming unfriendly. But I'm not going to walk around wearing a shirt that says *Tom*. Maybe I could just take the damn shirts and say thank you and throw them away in California.

"That's okay," he said, letting me off the hook. "I understand. You wanna retain your anonymity, right?"

"I guess so," I said, with a weak grin. His style was keeping me off balance.

Turning to Katharine, he said, "I don't have any Katharines, you know, that's one they missed. But I tell you what I *do* have. One of the smalls, won't fit me or anybody else around here, it says 'Ace.' You wanna be Ace?"

"I'd love to be Ace," Katharine said, and from the way she said it I knew she absolutely meant it.

"I'll drag it out for you in a little while." He looked over at the building, and the Checker was now inside. "First," he said, "let's go see what your trouble is."

As we walked across the blacktop I said, "That other fella. Is his name Jerry?"

"What? Naw, his *shirt's* named Jerry. He's named George."

"He answered to Jerry." I was feeling obscurely taken advantage of.

"Maybe he thought you were talking to the shirt," he said. "George is notoriously polite."

Inside, Jerry/George was just finished unhooking the towtruck from the front of the Checker. Ralph/Dave said to him, "After you park that, George, take a look in that box of shirts, behind the fan belts, see can you find the one called Ace."

"Okay, Dave," George said, and drove the towtruck out while Dave opened the cab's hood, pulled down a worklight on a retractable cable from the ceiling, hooked it on the hood so it shone down onto the engine, and then stood there brooding at the Checker's innards like an archaeologist trying to read a cave painting.

George soon found the Ace shirt, which Katharine put on over her own blouse, leaving it unbuttoned, and in which she looked absolutely wonderful. I have often envied women the wider range of wearing apparel permitted them by society; there have been windy days, for instance, when there was nothing more rational for me to wear on my head than a scarf, but even if I'd gone ahead and worn one (I never have) I know I wouldn't have looked wonderful in it, I'd simply have looked foolish. Katharine in her Ace shirt, though, looked so terrific I just wanted to stand there and gaze at her and smile, forever.

Well, almost forever. There is, in fact, nothing more boring in life than standing around on a concrete floor in some garage waiting for the mechanic to tell you what's wrong and how much it'll cost and how long it'll take and a lot of other things you don't really want to know, and a beautiful woman in a work-shirt named Ace can distract for only so long. Boredom which ends in enjoyment—waiting for a favorite TV program, for instance—is a lot more bearable than boredom which can only end badly. Katharine and I spent the next half hour walking around inside the garage, reading the wheel-alignment poster and the credit card information posters and the calendars and the oil filter poster and the ancient license plates nailed to the walls, and I was reduced to reading empty oil cans when at last Dave Smith came out from under the hood and said, "Tomorrow."

"That's what I was afraid of," I said.

"At the earliest," he added.

Katharine joined us, saying, "It can't be fixed today?"

"Sorry, Ace," Dave said. "It's the starter, all right, and we'll never get us a new one on a Sunday. Tomorrow morning, I'll call around, see what I can come up with. Even if we have to rebuild the old one here, we'll still need parts, and there's just no place to get them on a Sunday."

Katharine and I glanced at one another and shook our heads, and then Katharine said to Dave, "Would you mind explaining things to my fiancé?"

Dave looked at me, and it did me a world of good to see him nonplused for once. I just smiled and said not a word.

Katharine went on, saying, "I'll phone him now, all right?"

Dave didn't nonplus for long; you could see him figuring he'd catch up sooner or later. "Sure, Ace," he said. "I'll talk to any old body. The payphone's through there, in the office."

Dave and I remained in the garage long enough for me to give him a two-sentence capsule of our situation. He nodded through it, then frowned at the door through which Katharine had just gone. "That's funny," he said. "She don't seem the indecisive type. What's wrong with the fella?"

"I don't know, I've never met him."

He gave me a keen look. "You aren't an old friend or something."

"No, I'm just the cabdriver. I'm not part of the story at all."

He chuckled, with a knowing look, but before he could state his misconceptions and give me a chance to correct them the office door opened and Katharine appeared, somewhat nervous, saying, "Barry's on the phone. His name is Barry."

"His shirt is named Fred," I said.

Dave grinned at me, and went into the office with Katharine.

I stayed out by my fallen mount, looking with annoyance at the filthy innards under that raised hood. Katharine, of course, was pleased at anything that legitimately delayed our journey, but all I felt was irritated and upset. It was a strange reaction, really, since I was having just as good a time as Katharine and probably wanted the trip to end even less than she did, but that didn't mean I wanted us to *stop*. In some ways, this journey was like riding a bicycle; moving forward, no matter how erratically, made it possible to maintain our balance, but who knew what sort of fall would follow if we came to a complete halt? Getting derailed this way—to mix my transportation metaphors—put our relationship into a new and unknown pattern, which I could live without. I was becoming involved emotionally with Katharine—uselessly, pointlessly, ridiculously involved—and I was only too aware of what was happening, but so long as we maintained our original purpose together, this steady if slow progress westward, I could keep things under control. Given a day off, who would I turn out to be?

When Dave and Katharine returned, she was looking a little rattled but very relieved, and Dave was smiling like a man who'd love nothing more than to sit down with me over a beer and have a good long chat about the meaning of what he'd just been through. I believe he wanted to wink at me, but he didn't do it.

"Everything's all right," Katharine said. "Barry understands."

"Barry's a saint," I said.

She gave me a sharp look, then hurried on: "Dave says he'll drive us to the Holiday Inn."

"It's maybe a mile out," Dave explained, gesturing in a direction, "by the interstate exit. It's about the only place to stay in the general neighborhood."

"I'm sure it'll be fine," Katharine told me.

We walked back out to the sunlight, and over toward the disreputable looking automobiles. "I'll look for a new starter first thing in the morning," he said, "and call you at the hotel."

## 29

"Talk to you some time tomorrow, Tom," Dave said, as we and our luggage got out of his car. "Take it easy, Ace."

"Oh, I will," Katharine said, smiling at him, and he rattled away in his beat-up old Pontiac.

I said, "Do you want to be called Ace from now on?"

"Not by you," she said. "I like Dave to call me Ace because he really means it, but if you did you'd just be patronizing me."

How little people know one another. She couldn't have been more wrong just then, but if I tried to tell her the real attitude I'd have if I called her Ace I would get myself into very deep water indeed. So I just shrugged and said, "Katharine's a grand old name," and picked up my suitcase and one of hers, and she picked up her other suitcase, and we went into the Holiday Inn.

The young couple on duty at the desk in his-and-hers yellow blazers were having an affair; they were practically having it in our presence. They kept contriving to pass one another in the fairly narrow space behind the counter, rubbing against one another on the way by, giggling a little behind their hands, flashing one another conspiratorial, warning, forgiving looks. But they were efficient, I'll say that much for them; probably because the sooner they finished with us the sooner they'd be alone again. Also, their interest in one another was so total that it left them no awareness with which to become intrigued or baffled by our own fairly unusual relationship. We got our keys and our directions with no trouble, and found this time we'd been given adjoining but not connecting rooms.

And here it was again; the same room. I was getting so I

could find my way around this room blindfolded, I felt I knew it by now better than my own apartment back in New York. In a way it was becoming a sort of reassuring presence, this same room no matter where I went, but if I were going to be living in it very much longer I'd have to speak to the management about those non-Utrillos.

At the moment, however, my main problem was not highway art but time. It wasn't even three o'clock in the afternoon, and what on earth was I to do with myself? The day was sunny and the motel had a pool, but the air was too chilly for swimming. Without wheels, I couldn't go tour the sights of the neighborhood even presuming the neighborhood came equipped with sights. The hours between now and whenever tomorrow the cab would be fixed—oh, let it be tomorrow!—stretched ahead of me like a desert without oases. And all I had with which to defend myself was daytime TV and the four generations of the Gritbone family.

Political differences over the Spanish American War were pitting Gritbone brother against Gritbone brother when the phone rang. I looked at my watch, saw that the last twenty hours had used up barely fifteen minutes of real-world time, and knew this couldn't possibly be Dave with a reprieve. So it had to be Katharine.

It was. "I'm going crazy," she said.

I was in a grumpy enough mood to be ungracious: "Peace and quiet," I said. "It's very conducive to decision-making."

"Now, don't be mean."

I was immediately contrite: "Sorry, I guess I must be going crazy, too. Want to teach me chess?"

"Not a bit," she said. "I hate games with people who play worse than I do."

"Don't you like to win?"

"Of course, but only against real competition. Let's go for a walk."

"A what?"

"A walk," she repeated. "It's what we do with our feet when we go to dinner."

"I know what walk means. What I meant was, walk where?"

"Away from the motel. North maybe, or possibly south."

"Aha," I said. "I see what you mean."

"Glories of nature," she said.

"Take one's constitutional," I suggested. "Go for a hike."

"Stretch the legs. Get a lungful of fresh air."

"I'll knock on your door in one minute."

"I'll jog until you get here," she said.

## 30

When people think of Colorado they think of mountains; Denver, Boulder, Aspen, Vail, skiing, all that stuff. But that's all in the western half of the state, while we were still in eastern Colorado, which is every bit as flat as next-door Kansas. The mountains were visible far away to the west, blue-gray promises bunching on the horizon, but where we stood it was possible to see nothing much of interest in any direction at all for miles and miles and miles. No wonder they make science fiction movies in places like this; you're really aware that you're on a planet. And this is the landscape through which—no, *over* which—Katharine and I took our walk, heading arbitrarily north on the smallest available road, away from the Interstate.

It's a truism that we don't walk as much as we should, but behind the truism is the fact that we don't walk at *all*. By 'we' I mean Americans, but I probably mean Europeans and Canadians and South Americans and Japanese as well. Going from the garage to the house, or from the television set to the refrigerator, or even from the parking lot to the supermarket, isn't *walking*. In order to walk, you have to go somewhere you'd usually go by car—like two blocks for a newspaper.

Not that I took to this new experience right away. At first, my cantankerousness and boredom kept me from taking any interest or pleasure in what was happening, until suddenly I realized my body, all on its own, was enjoying itself. Our movement had achieved an easy strolling rhythm, our arms and legs were involved without strain, the dirt shoulder on which we strode was flat and even, there were no hills to contend with, traffic next to our left elbows was light, and it turned out that walking wasn't merely a method to get where you could do something else; walking was fun *in itself*. "This was a stroke of genius," I said.

Katharine beamed, then looked back and said, "See how far we've come already."

Not very far, actually, but that was all right; we had no appointments to keep. The Holiday Inn was a squat nodule in the near distance, among other low projections from the surface like groves of trees, clusters of barns, the town containing our cab, and some sort of factory westward with those water-cooling tanks that look like salt-and-pepper shakers.

Our road was old concrete, patched frequently with ragged scars of blacktop, traveled infrequently by mostly dusty cars and pick-up trucks. People looked at us in curiosity—nobody walks anymore—and one well-meaning fellow in a pick-up truck and cowboy hat stopped to ask if he could "help." We thanked him, assured him we could manage on our own, and he gave us a friendly smile, a big wave, and his wishes for good luck.

As we strolled, Katharine pointed out the various flora around us, bushes and trees and even some flowers here and there along the roadside, telling me what everything was called. I'm unredeemably a city boy; the names she quoted fell out of my head just as rapidly as she put them in. Still, it was nice to hear her talk about what was, after all, her subject, which led me at last to say, "What made you decide to be a landscape architect in the first place?"

She gave me a sidelong look: "What made you decide to be a cabdriver?"

"Oh, come on," I said. "Nothing, you know that. The only reason I'm driving a cab is because my father had one around the house. I take the path of least resistance. You don't. This whole journey is you taking the path of *most* resistance."

She laughed, then said, "Well, I usually take the path of least resistance, just like anybody else. I didn't start out wanting to be a landscape architect, it just happened."

"Sure."

"No, truly. When I was a little girl, what I wanted to be was a wife and a mommy, like everybody else. Then, around the time I went to college, the world opened up a little and it was all right to think of alternative futures, and then I decided what I wanted to be was personal secretary to a major politician, like a senator. Or maybe a movie executive. I was an American History major, with a Poli Sci minor, and I also learned shorthand and typing and all that, and when I graduated the placement office found me a job with a landscape architect."

"Oh, no!"

She was laughing at me. "Did you think I was a saint? Did you think I had a vocation?"

"Yes!" I gestured wildly yet vaguely, like Raggedy Andy. "That road of yours, those eight miles—"

She stopped, and turned, and looked at me very seriously. "That's one of the things you don't know, Tom," she said, "and it's probably why you're such a layabout."

"Thanks."

"You're welcome. You really believe, don't you, that a heavenly messenger has to appear in a circle of fire and tell you what to do with your life before you'll take any of it seriously. I *love* what I do, Tom, it uses whatever talents I have, it absorbs my interest, I think I'm very good at it; but until I got that secretarial job I didn't even know there *was* such a thing as a landscape architect. If I'd gone to work for a rug manufacturer instead, I'd probably be designing carpets at this very minute, and I'd most likely be pretty good at it."

"But don't landscape architects have to go to college for it and pass tests and things?"

"Of course," she said. "And I did, too, once I got involved. I'm fully accredited." She smiled, amused at the opportunity to shock me. "But the whole thing came from a three by five card in that placement office."

I clutched my brow. "Do you mean," I demanded, eyes widening, "that accident plays a significant part in human life? I don't think I can stand it."

She studied me from under lowered brows, as though I hadn't been joking. "No," she said thoughtfully, "I don't believe you can."

What terrible route the conversation might have taken from there I know not, because at that instant we were saved by the halting just beyond us of a black and gleaming Rolls Royce, out of which popped a tall lithe old woman in a lawn-party white dress, marcelled silver hair glistening in the sun, big cheerful smile on her lined and slender face as she called to us, "No more of that! You two just get in the car here and behave yourselves!"

## 31

"We're the Chasens," she said, half-turning in her seat so she could smile back at us as the Rolls rolled forward. "I'm Laura and this grim person at the wheel is Boyd."

"Delighted, I'm sure," said Boyd. In the rearview mirror his eyes seemed cheerful, not at all grim, behind round wire-framed glasses. As for what else I could see of him, his head was covered with a close-cropped layer of gray-white fuzz, his right shoulder was clad in pepper-and-salt tweed and his right ear was very clean. The car itself was lumpy and surprisingly small inside but comfortable, and smelled of oil and old leather.

"I'm Tom Fletcher," I said, to Laura's smiling face and Boyd's clean ear, "and this is Katharine Scott."

"There," Laura Chasen said, nodding at her husband. "Didn't I tell you, Boyd?"

"You certainly did, my dear." Boyd seemed perpetually amused by his wife's utterances.

Turning back to us, Laura said, "I knew you two weren't married, by the way you were arguing."

"We weren't arguing," I said.

"We were going for a walk," Katharine explained. "In fact, I'm not even sure why we got into this car."

"It's my wife's personality," Boyd assured her, complacently. "People simply do whatever she tells them, and then afterwards wonder how they got into such godawful jams."

"Now, don't turn these sweet people against me, darling," she said, in an offhand way, and leaned forward to take something out of the glove compartment, which she then extended over the back seat toward us. It was a smallish very attractive silver flask. "Care for a noggin?"

"No, thanks," I said. "Thank you very much."

She turned her bright smile on Katharine. "It's a martini," she said. "Excellent, excellent martini. Of course, you have to imagine the onion."

"Or the olive," offered Boyd.

"Exactly." Pleased, Laura patted Boyd's pepper-and-salt shoulder, while saying to Katharine, "That's the great advantage, you see, you can imagine it any way you want."

"Even lemon peel," suggested Boyd.

Laura made a face. "Absolutely not," she said. "Boyd, I forbid you to imagine lemon peel."

"Perhaps," Boyd said, his eyes crinkling with pleasure in the rearview mirror, "I'll imagine a big dollop of Rose's Lime Juice."

"Beastly man," Laura said, and held out the flask to Katharine. "Pay no attention to the Neanderthal, my dear. Just imagine a perfect tiny white cocktail onion, and have a little sip of this."

"It's a bit early in the day for me," Katharine said, hesitantly. I'd never seen her this tentative before. "I don't think I'm ready to drink just yet," she explained.

"Well," Boyd said, "you'd better be ready when we get there." Meantime, his wife was unscrewing the top from the flask.

"Where's that?" I asked.

"Max's," he said.

Laura took a ladylike sip, and a faint, sweet not unpleasant aroma of gin floated in the air. I could smell no vermouth at all. Recapping the flask, she explained, "It's a speak. Our favorite place in all the world."

"A speak?" I didn't get it. "You mean a speakeasy?"

"Let me warn you," Boyd said, "nothing pleases my wife more than the debauchery of the young."

I said, "I thought alcohol was legal in Colorado."

"Oh, it is," Laura said. "Max's is across the state line, in Kansas."

"There are still some counties in Kansas, I'm happy to say," Boyd told us, "that keep the banner of Prohibition flying."

"After all," Laura said, "what's the fun in drinking if it's legal?" Showing me the flask again, she said, "Sure you won't change your mind?"

When in Rome. "Well, maybe just a sip," I said.

"Mind you don't imagine lemon peel," she said, handing me the flask. It was very cold to the touch.

"You go ahead, Tom," Boyd said. "Your mind's your own, you can imagine whatever you want."

I imagined the vermouth.

## 32

"I have the feeling, Toto," Katharine whispered to me, "we're not in Oz anymore."

We sure weren't. Max's was a square low-ceilinged wooden room with too many support posts and an ineradicable smell of old beer. A functional but unlovely bar stretched across the back, and perhaps a dozen black formica tables with metal folding chairs were spotted around the rest of the place, leaving a scuffed central area available for dancing or knifefights. A dartboard hung on one side wall and a bowling machine and jukebox stood against the other. Even today's direct sunlight turned gray as it angled through the filthy plate glass windows in front, creating the impression of heavy cloud outside.

It was still rather early in the day for a place like this. In addition to our quartet—and we couldn't have looked more out of place here if we'd arrived by flying saucer—there were three stolid heavyset farmhands at the bar, drinking beer and talking about feed prices and politicians, plus another stolid heavyset farmhand behind the bar pretending to be the bartender. This fellow Boyd introduced to us as "my old pardner Farley," and Farley nodded at us with a half-sullen half-embarrassed little smile, as though he suspected he was somehow being made fun of; though it didn't seem to me that was Boyd's intention at all. Far from putting Farley down, I thought, Boyd was determined to lift him up, recreate him as an interesting tough guy in an exciting underworld setting. That neither Farley nor the establishment was capable of this pumpkin-to-coach transformation wasn't Boyd's fault; he was fairy-godmothering to beat the band.

As to Max himself, the owner of the place, Farley informed us he'd "gone down to Hays, comin back Tuesday, maybe Wednesday." In the meantime, Farley himself was just barely capable of dealing with the complexity of our drink orders; gin on the rocks for Laura, bourbon and water for Boyd, vodka and tonic for Katharine, and gin and tonic for me. We'd spent almost an hour in the Rolls Royce, so it was now nearly late enough for a drink anyway.

In that hour, the Chasens had told us so much about themselves that it was astonishing how little I actually knew. Boyd was seventy-four and "retired," but I had no idea what he was retired from. Laura was younger than her husband—she had girlish fun in keeping the exact number her own secret—and they'd been married fifty-two years, and had never been out of one another's sight. They'd also lived a lot of places; Greenwich Village in New York in the thirties and again in the late forties, San Francisco during the war years and again in the late fifties, Chicago in the early fifties, New Orleans for a while, London and Paris and Rome at odd moments, and even for six "bewildering" (Laura's laughingly expressed word) months in Rio de Janeiro. They had moved to Colorado five years ago, for unspecified medical reasons having to do with Boyd. Neither of them, however, looked in the least sickly, nor did either seem in the slightest concerned about illness.

"There," Laura said, as we settled around one of the formica tables with our drinks. "This is what I call a real joint."

"Depraved woman," Boyd said comfortably. "There was one time in Rome," he told us, "when only the sternest admonitions of the carabinieri kept this wife of mine from stripping to the buff and hurling herself into the Trevi Fountain."

"Narrow-minded man," retorted Laura. "What about the time in San Francisco when you rolled all those bowling balls down from Coit Tower?"

"You were amused at the time," he reminded her.

"I'm still amused," she told him, and turned to us, her big smile beaming as she said, "You can't imagine how funny that looked, all those bowling balls careening down that cobblestone street." Back to her husband, she said, "But you must admit it *was* childish, all the same."

"I'll admit no such thing," he told her, the perkiness of his manner taking the sting out of the words. "That was part of that experiment, if you'll remember, with Verner."

"Men," Laura decided, shaking her head in amusement, and sipped at her drink.

To me, Boyd said, "I take it you'll be traveling back this way, without your charming friend?"

"That's right," I said, surprised at the twinge the thought gave me, and almost equally surprised that Boyd had paid that much attention. Intermixed among their reminiscences and confidences in our hour together in the car had been a capsule explanation of our own journey together, which the Chasens had received more calmly than anybody else we'd talked to. They had treated it as though everyone they knew behaved in equally unusual ways all the time. In fact, Boyd had said, "Darling, wasn't it Phil Waterford took the cab from Chicago to New York with that singer?" "No, darling," she'd answered, "they went from Chicago to Boston. That was one of Phil Waterford's big failings." "What was?" Boyd had asked her. "That he took taxis?" "No," she'd answered, "that he persisted in going to Boston."

Now, Boyd told me, "You'll have to let us know when you'll be coming through, we'll lay on a little bash."

"What a lovely idea," said Laura, giving her husband a wide complimentary smile. "If there's one thing in life," she told Katharine and me, "that I love above all other things in life, it's a bash. And not a little one, either."

"You have to be watched, woman," Boyd said. "You have to be very carefully watched."

"Only when dancing," she corrected him, and looked over at the dance floor, her smile not quite buried by a thoughtful frown. "Boyd, darling," she said, "I don't hear any music."

"I do, darling," he said, "every time you speak." And reaching into his pocket he pulled out a lot of change.

"Poo," Laura said, brushing away the compliment with negligent fingers. "That isn't music. What I want is hot licks."

"And you shall have them." Smiling at Katharine and me, Boyd said to his wife, "What say we give these youngsters a treat?"

"Not your owl imitations, dear."

Astonishingly, Boyd grabbed my hand and plunked three quarters into the palm, saying, "You two go study that jukebox. Play whatever strikes your fancy."

"But—" I couldn't believe those quarters. "I don't know what you'd want to hear."

"Don't worry about it, Tom," he said. "You just go over there—you, too, Katharine—and see what you see."

There seemed to be some extra significance, some *comic* extra significance, in this suggestion, but on the other hand there was an aura of comic extra significance about everything these two said. "Well," I told him, getting to my feet, "you're the first person ever to trust my musical judgment. Be warned." And belatedly realized I'd started talking like *them*. "Come on, Katharine," I said, resisted additional comments about tripping the light fantastic, and we crossed the room together to the jukebox.

Where we learned the reason for that extra significance. The jukebox, which I'd expected to be stocked with country & western, or even country disco—John Denver at the very *best* —was choc-a-bloc with golden oldies. But I mean *really* golden oldies. On the radio, a golden oldie is some miserable turkey barely two years old, but what this jukebox was filled with was big bang swing from the thirties and forties. Duke Ellington, Woody Herman, Bunny Berigan, Ray McKinley, Billie Holiday with Teddy Wilson, on and on and on.

Standing over this cornucopia, Katharine and I had our first opportunity for private comment since the Chasens had collected us, and I began it by saying, "You think they're sweet."

"I do not," she said. "Maybe I think they're scary. Are they pushing very hard, or is it natural?"

"Maybe forty years ago they pushed very hard," I suggested, "but now I think it's natural."

"Do you have the feeling," she asked, "that a lot of famous people lurk in the background of those stories?"

"You mean, they're very specifically not name-dropping? Yeah, I had the same impression." Slotting one of Boyd's quarters, I made a selection, and Artie Shaw's *Begin the Beguine* began to wander like a lost soul around this terrible room.

"But why are they *here*?" Katharine asked. "They have money, they're sophisticated, they've lived all over the world."

"Health problems."

"This is the only spot on Earth with the right climate?"

More quarters, more selections. Shrugging, I said, "I guess it's the only spot with the right climate *and* a handy speakeasy."

Boyd and Laura had started dancing, a bit stiffly but with a lot of élan, and Farley was putting more drinks on the table when we got back to it. Farley gave us a sheepish grin and said, "They're nice people."

"This ought to be my round," I said, though my first drink was barely touched.

"It's mine," Farley said, picked up Boyd and Laura's empty glasses, and went back behind his bar. The other three customers watched the Chasens dance, simple smiles on their honest faces. Katharine and I sat sipping our first drink till our host and hostess returned to the table, with Glenn Miller's *Little Brown Jug* beginning to churn in the background. Both of them had somewhat high color, and seemed well pleased with themselves. Boyd grinned at me: "Well? Find anything there you like?"

"As a jukebox," I said, "I consider it a major national asset."

"Good man."

Laura rested a feather-light hand on my forearm. "Tell me the truth, Tom," she said, seeming unusually serious. "Did you notice Clyde McCoy's *Sugar Blues* on that machine?"

"Yes, I did."

"Did you play it?"

"No."

"Good." Patting my arm, she told her husband, "We can keep him."

"We'll have to keep them both," Boyd said. "They're a matched set."

Katharine laughed, surprising me very much. "You two *are* wonderful," she said.

"Of course we are," Laura told her. Somehow, her glass was empty again. "Boyd, darling," she said. "Let's pub-crawl."

"Your restlessness never ceases to amaze me," he said. His glass was also empty. Rising, he said, "Come along, you two, help me restrain this woman's wilder impulses." And he turned to call, "So long, pardner!" to Farley, who offered in return his hesitant smile, plus a small wave from a filthy bar rag. On the jukebox, *Little Brown Jug* gave way to Count Basie's *One O'Clock Jump*.

I said, "Our drinks aren't finished." They weren't, in fact, started.

"Bring them along," Boyd said. "Farley doesn't mind."

"Yoo hoo!" Laura cried. "Farr-lee! We're stealing your glasses!"

Another smile, another pass of the rag, and this time a nod as well.

So we took our glasses.

# 33

It's hard to pub-crawl in western Kansas and eastern Colorado, particularly if you're trying to limit yourself to speakeasies, but the Chasens managed it surprisingly well. Most of the joints we hit were legal bars, if the truth be known, but they all at least *looked* disreputable, and as the afternoon wore on into evening they began to fill up with a clientele to match. In a place called the Polka Bar, with pale green concrete block walls, one burly monster in a leather jacket offered to punch Boyd out for some obscure reason of his own, but Laura laughed so gaily, and fluttered her hands so uncaringly, and said so many ineffable words so fast that the lout found himself somehow dancing with the wife rather than fighting with the husband; Boyd's only voiced reaction, watching them swirl away across the crowded dance floor, was, "What low taste that woman has. How she wound up with me I will never know." Within a minute she was back, flushed and buoyant, kissing Boyd on the cheek and saying, "Such fun places you bring me to! Where shall we go next?"

Somewhere in through there we had dinner, in a ramshackle restaurant completely covered with shingles, inside and out. It was like eating in a lumberyard, an image encouraged by the chef's apparent use of sawdust as a thickener in the sauces. This chef, Tony, a squat gnarled villainous older man with two missing fingers and a lot of aggressive tattoos, came out to talk voluble Italian with Boyd, who seemed to handle himself moderately well in the language; at least he made Tony laugh a lot, while Laura explained to us that they'd known Tony for years, since before he'd quit the sea: "He was chef on several yachts. Why he came to this dry place, with nary a squid nor a shrimp in sight, is one of life's most baffling mysteries." My coq au vin wasn't very good, but Tony had proudly presented us with two bottles of bardolino—his treat—which turned out to be the softest and gentlest Italian wine I'd ever tasted, so I couldn't call the meal a total loss.

Around midnight, Katharine and I started making noises about going home, but our hosts wouldn't hear of it. We were just barely moving into the realms of the after-hours joint, a more modern and therefore more plentiful sort of speakeasy. And so the gay round continued; we'd drive for ten or twenty minutes, we'd pull in at some half-full gravel parking lot next to some unprepossessing roadhouse, we'd enter to a flurry of greetings—the Chasens were known everywhere we went—and we would then drink or eat or both on the Chasens' tab. Several times I tried reaching for a check, but Boyd and the waiters maintained a conspiracy against me. Once I quit being guilty and embarrassed about such behavior, I rather enjoyed it.

We had left a place called the Tick Tock, and were entering the Rolls under the harsh glare of a parking lot floodlight, when Boyd made a strangling sound, stiffened, and fell face down across the front seat, absolutely rigid, legs sticking out of the car behind him. Awful rasping noises came from his throat, and his fingers scratched like little dying insects against the leather of the seat, but otherwise he was a block of wood. Laura, about to enter the car on the other side and finding Boyd's head there on the seat, clucked and said, "Now, isn't that just like a man. Boyd, I can't think where you get this taste for melodrama. Tom, would you be a darling and turn poor Boyd over?" During all of which speech she was briskly opening the glove compartment, removing from it a smallish zippered leather bag, and opening the zipper to reveal a compartmented interior filled with tubes and bottles and a hypodermic syringe.

I ran around to the driver's side, grabbed Boyd by the thighs and found his flesh quivering beneath my hands; more like a machine vibrating than a person. I wrestled him onto his back, while Laura prattled on in her careless way, little comments about Boyd thinking of no one but himself, plus interpolated directions to me: "Just loosen his tie, Tom. Oh, I suppose you might as well unbutton the collar, too."

Boyd's face was gray-blue in that glaring light, and his eyes bulged from their sockets. Instructing Katharine to push up Boyd's left sleeve, Laura reached down with those feathery fingers of hers—but now they seemed fingers of thin steel—forced Boyd's rigid jaws apart, inserted a wooden ice cream stick between his blue-black lips, commenting, "If you swallow that tongue, my darling, you won't like it at all, and don't say I never warned you."

Katharine, beside me as she struggled with the sleeves of Boyd's jacket and shirt, was wide-eyed with shock; her breath rasped in her throat almost as badly as Boyd's himself. I continued to hold Boyd's legs, uselessly, and watched as Laura filled the syringe from one of the small bottles, found the vein in Boyd's arm, and gave him a brisk injection. And chatted away all the time: "You might as well have done this at the table, much more convenient and I never did like that place anyway. Come to think of it, I've always had something against ginmills called Tick Tock. All that hurry hurry hurry, clock watching, efficiency experts. What was that song in *Pajama Game*? Oh, Boyd, you remember, Mimi sang it that time when Sammy played the piano. Tempus fugit? Oh, I suppose it's just as well my memory's so bad, or that's what *you'd* say."

Meantime, Boyd was indeed trying to say something. The

injection had had an immediate effect, relaxing his rigid muscles, making it possible for him to breathe again, in great gulping raspy painful-sounding gasps, through which—with that wooden stick in his mouth—he was trying to speak. Vague thoughts of last words floated in my mind as I leaned forward over his supine body, saying, "What? Boyd?"

"Somebody—" Breath rattled in his chest, his eyes still bulged, it was obviously a terrible strain to speak at all. His hand very shakily crawled up over his chest to his face, and clumsily removed the wooden stick. "Somebody," he told me, showing me the stick, "stole my Popsicle."

"Oh, Boyd," Laura said, in the amused long-suffering tone of the indulgent mother, "you just never take anything seriously at all. I just don't know what to do with you." She was efficiently repacking the medicine kit, having shaken two white capsules from one of the little bottles into her palm. "Here," she said, extending these capsules negligently toward him. "Sit up like a good boy and take your pills. Wash them down with some martini."

He was so weak, so filled with pain, that great hobnails of perspiration stood out on his forehead and a rank odor of sick sweat rose up from his body, but he struggled with utter determination to sit up. I helped him, and he got into a normal seated position, propping himself with both forearms on the steering wheel. "Depraved woman," he gasped, blinking straight ahead. "Capsules with martini? Have you no white wine?"

"You'll just have to rough it, my dear."

"I might have married Theodora Lind," he said. "She was soft."

"Mostly in the head, sweetheart. Here, take your pills, we have bars to go before we sleep."

"For mercy's sake, don't repeat it."

"Bars to go before we sleep," she said, with a wicked smile, and watched him fondly as he swallowed the two white capsules with a long swig from the silver flask.

Katharine, the tremor in her voice belying her attempt at casualness, said, "As a matter of fact, I don't think Tom and I do have bars to go before we sleep. Are we anywhere near the Holiday Inn?"

Boyd looked at us, eyes glazed and face puffy but expression benign. "Oh, don't be quitters," he said. "The night's a pup."

"Then I'm a fire hydrant," I said. "It's been a wonderful evening, but Katharine and I are both pretty worn out by now, and we have a lot of driving to do tomorrow."

"Miles to go *after* we sleep," Katharine said.

Boyd looked at her in mock horror. "Are you going to repeat that?"

"Are you going to take us home?"

"I tell you what," Laura said. "There's a lovely hoochery right on our way. We'll just stop there for a quick good night drink, and then it's off to the Holiday Inn. All right?"

That was the best deal we were going to get. "Fine," I said. "Thank you." Then I frowned at Boyd. "Are you all right to drive?"

He reared up with comic dignity; most of the effects of the attack had worn off by now, though he was till sweaty and shaky. "Do you mean to suggest," he demanded, "that I might be a bit the worse for drink?"

That had not been at all what I'd meant to suggest, and he knew it as well as I did. "You know best," I said, and held the door for Katharine to re-enter the car.

# 34

The final forty minutes with the Chasens were the strangest of all. Never for a second did their characterizations slip, did their play-acting lapse; what had happened had not happened, nothing had changed, there were no clouds in their sky, there was nothing but frivolousness and nonchalance. They were merely amused by one another, and not terribly involved together emotionally at all.

Our job was to agree with this view, to play along, and we did it to the hilt. We were probably brighter and more bubbly in that final bar, Katharine and I, than we'd been all evening. The strain was severe, but if Laura and Boyd could take it, by God, so would we.

Laura, in that last bar, wrote their names and address and phone number on the backs of two beer-label coasters, writing in a clear tiny firm hand with black ink, then presenting one coaster to each of us as though they were door prizes. I promised faithfully to get in touch on my return trip, and I wondered if I would. Katharine promised just as faithfully to call if and when her work ever brought her back to this part of the world.

I don't know if they realized how difficult we found it to go on playing the game, but they put up only token resistance when we refused a second drink in that last bar and insisted we absolutely had to return to the motel. Still as cheerful as ever, they drove us to the Holiday Inn, where as we got out Boyd said, "I want to thank you both for helping me protect my wife from her baser impulses. You can see it isn't easy."

"Our pleasure," I assured him.

"Boyd won't be content," Laura said comfortably, "until I'm walled up in a convent somewhere. Thank you both for bringing a little color into my tragic life."

The Rolls drove off, and we stood in the parking lot to wave after it until it turned onto the highway and the red taillights disappeared. Then our hands lowered to our sides. "Good God," Katharine said.

I didn't feel like saying anything at all. We went up to our rooms and Katharine stopped at her door, saying, "Good night."

"Good night."

"Do you know what's the most terrible thing of all?" she asked.

I had walked on, toward my own room. I looked back. "What?"

"They love each other," she said.

## 35

It had been a long exhausting night. I left no call, and didn't wake up till nearly ten o'clock. My first act was to phone Smith's Svce, where Dave Smith answered with his usual greeting: "*More* trouble."

"No, the same old trouble, actually," I told him. "This is Tom Fletcher, the cabby."

"The ex-cabby."

"Don't talk like that," I said. "My stomach just dropped."

"Well," he said, "I've got a line on a Marathon starter, over in Limon. It's probably gonna be a little different from yours, but maybe we can cobble them together, come up with some cockamamie thing. At least get you off my hands and over the county line."

"That sounds good."

"Give me a call about one o'clock," he suggested.

I said, "Checkout here is twelve noon."

"Tell them a sob story."

"It just happens I have one, as a matter of fact."

He chuckled, and we stopped talking to one another, and I phoned Katharine's room, thus learning what she sounded like when first awake; warm and nice, but brain-damaged. "Wo," she said. "Zat?"

"It's the morning after."

"God. Oh, it sure is. What time is it?"

"Ten."

"Ten what? Oh, ten o'clock; I'm sorry, I'm not waking up."

"They may stop serving breakfast pretty soon."

"That's one good thing."

"I'll knock on your door in ten minutes."

"You're a vicious person," she said, but when I knocked on her door ten minutes later she'd reconstructed herself and seemed fine. She was wearing her Ace shirt, and I found myself glad she hadn't been wearing it last night, because I knew instinctively she would have let the Chasens call her Ace. It still rankled that she wouldn't permit the same privilege to me.

During breakfast we talked about the car and Dave Smith and what on earth we would do between now and one o'clock. Looking at me doubtfully, she said, "Just how bad a chess player are you?"

"I know which way the horse goes."

She sighed, but accepted the inevitable, and after breakfast we sat out in the cool sunlight by the swimming pool and Katharine laid out her neat black-and-white traveling chess set with the magnetic pieces. "I'll bet a quarter Barry gave you this," I said. "Wait a minute, wait a minute, not for Christmas. Your birthday."

"Smart aleck. Let's see how smart you are at chess."

So we played for a while, just sort of moving the pieces around ineffectually, and then she said, "I couldn't get to sleep last night. I kept thinking about the Chasens."

"That was very strange," I agreed.

"Early on, I said maybe I found them scary. I was right." She looked away, out over the swimming pool toward the big trucks passing on the Interstate; she was apparently having trouble finding the words for what she wanted to say. "I took it personally," she said.

"I don't follow."

"I connected it with Barry and me." She looked in my direction, squinting a bit, troubled. "You know what they reminded me of?"

"What?"

"William Powell and Myrna Loy in *The Thin Man*." Then she shook her head, saying, "No, that's not exactly it. All his pretending his wife is this crazed wanton, this nymphomaniac or something, that was more like Thorne Smith. I'm not making any sense, am I?"

"Not that I can tell."

"It's a strategy for dealing with intimacy," she said. "Do you see what I mean? At the time they started out together, the Chasens, back in the twenties and thirties, that was one of the role models you could follow for a relationship. You just stayed on the surface together, being amusing, appreciating one another's wit and not taking anything seriously. Because marriage, or any real intimacy between people, it can be very frightening."

"As you well know," I said.

"As I well know," she agreed. "Ten years ago, the popular strategy was to stay stoned together, laid back, cool. People are always trying to find the right strategy."

I said, "And you're afraid you haven't found the right strategy for you and Barry."

"It's worse than that," she said. "I'm not even sure I want to get into the strategy thing at all. That's why they were so scary, they're stuck in that role, they've got no place else to go. And look what they have to make it adapt to; old age, sickness. God knows what their real story is and why they have to be out here, pretending awful Kansas bars are Broadway joints out of Damon Runyon."

"At one point last night," I said, "I found myself wondering how they are when alone."

"Exactly the same," she said, with utter certainty. "They weren't doing all that for us, they were doing it for one another.

*They're* the audience. And they can't ever break out of it, because once out they'd never get back in, and they'd have nobody to be together. Sooner or later one of them will die, and the other one will make a joke about it."

"Jesus," I said. "You do have grim thoughts."

"I was thinking about Barry. Barry and me." She looked down at the chessboard, and sighed, and slowly focused her attention on the game. "Mate in three moves," she said.

"Yeah?" I looked down at the tangle of pieces. "Which of us wins?"

## 36

George's shirt today was named Howard. It made him seem more formal, somehow, more a serious person. Being separated from his towtruck also helped. He came out to the Holiday Inn to pick us up about two-thirty, driving another disreputable automobile, this one a Ford station wagon with half the chrome ripped off and a lot of shock absorbers and stray pieces of metal in the back. Around noon I'd told my sob story to the lovers at the front desk, and they'd agreed to keep our luggage behind the counter until we could leave; following which we'd eaten a cardboard lunch and then sat around the pool some more, me semi-immersed in Gritbone woes and Katharine alternately leafing through magazines and snoozing. Neither of us suggested taking a walk; I think we were both afraid we might have an adventure.

Then, a little after two, I was called to the desk for a phone call, and it was Dave Smith: "Well, she's running, for the moment. Better get here and take her away before she quits. I'm sending George to pick you up."

And so he did. And it was in the grungy back seat of the Ford, on the way to Smith's Svce, that Katharine informed me she still wanted to do the detour business we'd talked about yesterday. "It makes just as much sense today as it did then," she pointed out.

"That's right," I said. "And yesterday it made no sense at all."

"Barry agreed to it."

"That was before we broke down and lost a day."

"He agreed," she insisted. "And you agreed. And I agreed.

And I still want a day away from that highway. Just one day, Tom."

So did I—the memory of Kansas and that afternoon sun was still fresh in my mind—but I felt a certain obligation to our ostensible purpose. "You'll have to check with Barry," I said.

She was outraged. "I will not! Tom, that isn't fair, you're hiding behind Barry. I talked with him yesterday, and he agreed, and that's enough."

I went on arguing until I became aware of George's amused eyes watching me in the rearview mirror. Plainly, he knew I was beaten and he was wondering when I'd figure it out for myself and lie down. "Oh, very well," I said, getting grumpy mainly because I felt like an idiot in front of George, which was of course an idiotic reason to feel grumpy, which made me grumpier, "very very well, have it your own way."

"I intend to."

"We'll take an unreliable vehicle that's already broken down once and we'll go haring off into the wilderness over a lot of dirt roads and ski trails."

"That's right," she said. The damn woman wouldn't even fight with me.

Dave Smith was waiting for us out by his gas pumps, wearing a shirt called Al. "Hi, Ace," he said. "You wearing that shirt on my account?"

"On mine," she assured him. "I think I look terrific in it."

"You do." Turning to me, he said, "Shall we see if my bubble gum repair job still works?"

"I'm looking forward to it."

He was being laconic, but I could sense that in fact he was quite pleased with himself. Apparently he'd performed some sort of mechanical wizardry with the original starter plus parts from the other one. In any event, we walked together into the garage, where the cab awaited, looking stocky and inappropri-ately smug, and Dave had me start and stop the engine a dozen times, and it worked fine. His good humor lasted even into the question of payment, when it turned out he recognized no known credit card but would take my personal check on a New York City bank. I stared at him: "You will?"

"Anybody who crosses America in a Checker cab is too dumb to be a thief," he said. "Make it out to Smith's Svce." So I did.

Katharine sat up front with me, and Dave stood smiling in the sunlight, rubbing dirt into his hands from an oily orange rag, as we drove out of the garage. "Good luck," he called.

"We'll need it," I answered. "We're going cross-country from here."

# 37

It was somewhere west of Castle Rock that we got lost. "I don't want to say I told you so," I said.

"Good," said Katharine. "I'm glad you don't. Something called Santa Maria is supposed to be down this way."

"Now we're looking for ghost ships."

We were not in a good mood. I was pilot and Katharine was navigator, and the best you can say for us is that we managed not to go to Denver, though that was the only place mentioned with any consistency on the road signs we saw. We kept firmly turning the opposite way every time we came to one of those signs, and according to the sun peeking at us over the tops of the mountains we were managing to keep our nose pointed more or less westward.

The countryside had changed. Ever since western Kansas there had been a gradual rising trend in the landscape, but it wasn't until about forty miles after we'd abandoned Route 70 that the distant blue mountains on the western horizon suddenly became green, huge, and *present*. Up we climbed, up and up, the cab curving up mountain roads it had never even dreamed of in the canyons of New York. The broken forested land was beautiful, had I been in a mood for beauty, but it wasn't exactly rapid or easy going, and not for a second did I find myself getting bored at the steering wheel.

We never did find Santa Maria. We also failed to find Montezuma, Breckenridge, Como, Climax, and Leadville. Katharine even alleged at one point that we were about to come upon a placed called Fairplay. We didn't, of course.

Tempers were fraying. A certain amount of bickering took place, each of us making unkind and unwelcome statements, of the sort it's just as well not to dwell on afterward, and then at a given point we both simply stopped talking. We fumed side by side, enclosed in our separate senses of outrage, and I picked my way over through the mountains following the scanty hints and clues of the road signs.

It was in no town at all that I came around a curve and saw an old board sign up ahead reading *Tourist Cabins*. It was now about six-thirty, and most of the time we were driving in increasingly obtuse shade, since the sun was now definitely on the other side of the mountains. I said, "Katharine, I don't care what you want, that's where we're staying. In the morning they can loan us some sled dogs to lead us back to civilization."

"Good," she said, tightlipped.

Behind the tourist-cabin sign was a small white clapboard structure, itself more a cabin than a real house. OFFICE, said a magic-marker notice on a shirt-cardboard thumbtacked to the front door. I stopped the cab and Katharine got out and slammed the door very hard.

She was in the OFFICE quite a long while, and when she came out she was accompanied by a gnarled skinny tall old man bent by arthritis but nevertheless spry. His white shirt and gray workpants were both far too large. He gestured to me to follow him down the gravel driveway beside the house; in his hand was a pair of big keys attached to big pieces of wood. Katharine didn't look in my direction.

Behind the house were eight separate little tourist cabins spaced in a long crescent with the gravel drive running past them in front. We were apparently the only customers at the moment. The old man led the way—for no particular reason that I could see—to the third cabin from the right, and gestured to me to pull the cab in beside it, which I did. I got out and opened the trunk while he was unlocking the cabin. He pushed the door open, then came over to me and said, "Howdy do."

"Hello."

"That's the young lady's cabin," he said, "and yours is this one." Pointing to the cabin on the other side of the cab.

"Okay."

"Here's the key. The lock's a little tricky, but just jiggle it. Can you carry your own bags?" He had clear very pale blue eyes and thin-looking parchment skin.

"Oh, I think so."

"Which are the young lady's bags?"

I gave them to him, got out my own, closed the trunk lid and went away to my cabin. I was still jiggling the key in the lock when he came over and said, "Having trouble?"

"Oh, no. Just with this door here."

"Let me show you." He did, then locked the door again and had me try it myself, using his method. It worked. "You'll be all right now," he said.

"I'm sure I will. Thank you."

Inside the cabin was the smell of wood. The walls were unfinished rough lumber and the floor was pine planking. The double bed—brass headboard and footboard—had a scratchy-looking Indian-patterned wool blanket over it. The furnishings were a sagging gray mohair armchair, a dark brown metal bureau, a white-edged mirror hanging from a nail, a square maple bedside table with a drawer, a red-shaded table lamp upon this, an amber-shaded floor lamp over by the chair, and a huge sepia print of "The Return From Calvary" over the bed. No non-Utrillos.

When I dropped my bag on the bed the springs squeaked, loudly. So I sat on it and, as expected, it was as lumpy as bad mashed potatoes. Also as soft. I stood again and pulled open the narrow unpainted door in the rear wall and looked in at the smallest bathroom in the Western Hemisphere. The toilet wasn't *quite* under the sink, which was crammed in next to the free-standing white metal shower. Linoleum on the floor, linoleum in a fake tile pattern on the walls. The narrow window over the sink was covered by a dark red curtain; when I pushed it to one side to look out I saw a close-up view of a lot of pine trees.

The worst thing about a fight is the difficulty in backing out of it. I would have liked to chat with Katharine about this place, comparing it with our usual Holiday Inn, and I suppose she would have liked to discuss it with me as well, but we couldn't talk about anything pleasant because we weren't talking to one another at all; having talked a bit too much *at* one another when we were angry. Nobody wants to be the first to extend the olive branch, in case the other guy is still in a chainsaw mood.

I unpacked some things from my bag, then sat on the lumpy scratchy uncomfortable mohair chair for about ten minutes, trying to read my saga, but finally gave up and went outside, just for something to do. Also I'd had this vague hope that Katharine might coincidentally be outside at the same moment; conversation could ensue, we could get back on the old footing, and I could say my one or two funny things about the cabin. I was absolutely choking with my undelivered funny remarks about the cabin.

She wasn't outside.

I went over to look at the cab, but there wasn't a heck of a lot there to occupy my attention. Then I noticed a narrow dirt path winding away into the woods from behind the cabins, and I strolled in that direction, feeling the slightly cool dampness of the forest air, smelling that nice acrid aroma of pine tree. It really was beautiful country; no place to be in a bad mood.

I walked on through the trees, diagonally down a gradual slope, surrounded by the hushed chatter of woods creatures. Brown pine needles made a blanket/carpet/layer in which all sounds were muted. When I looked back, the white tourist cabins were no longer visible through the trees.

The path bifurcated, and I took the fork to the right, the one that went more steeply downhill. I felt the need for exercise, for some use of my body that would counteract all that time in the cab. Walking in the woods was clearing my head of everything; road fatigue, bad temper, uneasiness of spirit.

There was something ahead. A road? A building? It seemed to me I could faintly hear the struggling roar of a big truck climbing a hill. I kept walking, and saw a clearing ahead, and abruptly stepped out at the top of a cleared grassy hillside; and there was the road. A major road, in fact, Route 70 or some other Interstate, making a broad gray double-scar slice across the haunch of a mountain.

And a Holiday Inn! On the far side of the road, there it was, two stories high and red brick and sprawled out in all directions, the biggest Holiday Inn in the *world*. By God, we could be there in five minutes!

I stood looking at it, thinking about the air-conditioning and the perfect double bed and the expansive bathroom and the perfectly acceptable restaurant, and also thinking about the tourist cabin's lumpy bed and awful mohair armchair and tiny tin shower—and the smell of wood and the proprietor's very pale clear eyes—and I didn't know what to do. When I finally turned away I was still a mass of confusion, in which only one thing was clear; I could certainly talk to Katharine about *this*.

I walked quickly back through the woods, this time paying no attention to my surroundings, and when I got back to the cabins I saw that Katharine's door was standing open. Was that a peace sign? I stood outside and said, "Knock knock."

Her voice came from within: "Who's there?"

"Albee."

"Albee who?"

"Albee down to getcha in a taxi, honey."

She came to the door and grimaced. "Did you just make that up?" She wasn't angry anymore.

Neither was I. "I think so," I said.

"Are there going to be any more like that?"

"Not right away."

"Then you can come in."

"Thank you." And I knew I wasn't going to tell her about the Holiday Inn. I *wanted* to stay here, lumpy bed and all. It was better that she not know we had an alternative.

Her cabin was completely different from mine, but exactly the same, if you know what I mean. It had been furnished out of the same attic. "Ah," I said. "You have the Grover Cleveland suite."

"Mr. Hilyerd says John Dillinger stayed here one time."

"He's probably still in Cabin Six."

"About food," Katharine said, and my heart sank: we would drive around looking for a restaurant, we would discover the Holiday Inn. I said, "Yes?"

"If we want supper around seven-thirty, *Mrs.* Hilyerd will be happy to make it for us. Do we like steak, corn on the cob, baked potato, green beans, and apple pie?"

I said, "Would you repeat the question?"

## 38

Mrs. Hilyerd, a woman as rangy and bony as her husband, was the sort of cook who believes food should taste like itself. We sat in a small enclosed porch at the rear of their house, which had been furnished with three completely non-matching tables and a whole lot of chairs that had nothing in common except one or two slats missing out of their backs, while Mrs. Hilyerd served us herself, on heavy china dishes featuring handpainted crabapples on a cream ground. The food was so delicious that I just kept eating everything I saw; Mrs. Hilyerd can consider herself lucky I didn't take a bite out of her hand.

We had neither wine nor liquor, but with such food alcohol would have been an excess. "We're Temperance," Mrs. Hilyerd had explained, "but we don't push our views on others. If you have a bottle and you want empty glasses…" When we assured her we had no bottle, she filled the glasses with crisp icy water from a jug she kept in the refrigerator.

At the end of the meal, to put a metaphor in precisely the wrong place, she spilled the beans. Watching, with pardonable satisfaction, as we engulfed her hot apple pie (with cheese slices), she said to Katharine, "You won't get a pie like that over to the Holiday Inn."

"No, I'm sure I won't," Katharine said, looking guilty. I stared at her, and she became very absorbed in slicing a bit of cheese with the side of her fork.

Mrs. Hilyerd went back to the kitchen. From deeper in the house came the rattle of canned laughter; Mr. Hilyerd watching television. I sipped my glass of water and said, "You *knew* about the Holiday Inn."

"Mr. Hilyerd told me, when we first got here." She looked at me with a tentative smile. "He said he gives everybody the choice, he doesn't want to take advantage of people just because they're lost."

"But you decided to stay."

"I thought, if we went to the Holiday Inn, the fight would last longer."

"Katharine," I said, "I know I shouldn't say this, but there are times when I wish I was Barry, and this is one of them."

"Eat your pie," she said. "You don't want to hurt Mrs. Hilyerd's feelings."

So I ate my pie, grinning at her while chewing, until all at once she put her fork down, frowned across the table at me, and said, "*Wait* a minute."

Oh oh. I drank water and looked as innocent as possible. "Mmm?"

"*You* knew about the Holiday Inn."

"I took a walk out behind the cabins," I admitted. "I saw it."

"Is it *that* close?"

"I'm afraid so."

She looked at me, very sternly, and then she began to grin. "I know what I shouldn't say," she told me, "and I'm not going to say it."

Mrs. Hilyerd appeared in the doorway: "More pie?"

## 39

After dinner we were invited to watch television with the Hilyerds in their small cramped living room, which had been furnished from an attic twenty years newer than the one that had supplied the cabins. Mr. Hilyerd preferred situation comedies heavy with canned laughter. His wife from time to time would stand in the doorway to watch, then shake her head and make a comment about "foolishness" and go back to the kitchen.

At ten o'clock Mr. Hilyerd yawned, rose, switched off the TV set, and said, "Good night. Don't let the bedbugs bite."

I said, "You already fed them, eh?"

He gave me a sharp look while he caught up, then said, "Heh. Heh."

We went out through the kitchen. Mrs. Hilyerd said, "Breakfast about seven-thirty?"

"That'd be fine," Katharine said. "Would you call us at seven?"

"I'll bang on the door. Doors." Which was the only indication she ever gave that she found our status unconventional.

There were stars out, millions of them, very high and tiny in the soft black sky, and the moon was one night rounder. By its light we crunched over the gravel drive to our cabins. We stopped together out front. "Katharine," I said. "Jesus Christ, Katharine."

But she shook her head, saying, "No. This is a dream and you know it."

"Let's stay asleep."

She smiled, saying she also wanted to. "I'll see you in the morning, Tom."

The bed was lumpy and I could neither sleep nor read my saga. At two in the morning I took a long hot shower, and some time after three I fell asleep, with the light on.

## 40

Noon, and we were at a baking Texaco station somewhere in Utah, talking to Barry on the phone. The receiver was almost too hot to touch, and when I held it to my face sweat droplets formed all around my ear, under my hair.

This was the worst day of the trip. The dream had ended with a vengeance. I'd awakened at seven to the thumping of Mrs. Hilyerd's bony fist on the door, and I'd known at once some point of no return had been reached last night. Critical mass, flashpoint, whatever the right image would be; Katharine and I could no longer glide effortlessly along together, that's all. No more sidetrips, no more delays; I had to get her to Los Angeles as fast as humanly possible, and *end* this thing.

When I entered the enclosed porch for breakfast I saw at once from Katharine's face that she'd reached the same understanding. The pressure at the table with us was so intense that afterward I couldn't remember what I'd eaten; which is undoubtedly a shame, given Mrs. Hilyerd's class as a cook. We ate, Katharine paid, we loaded the cab, the Hilyerds came out to wave us goodbye, and we drove silently to Route 70. Katharine rode up front with me, but I think that was only because the tension would have become even more blatant if she'd sat in the back.

Interstate 70 is discontinuous through western Colorado, so from time to time we were dumped onto US 6 for several miles, a slower and narrower road, where the slow-moving big rigs crawling through the endless curving hilly no-passing zones came very close to snapping my taut brain. On the existing stretches of 70 I floored the accelerator, and the poor cab quivered as I strained it at the very limit of its capacity. If my father had seen me, he'd have torn out his last six hairs.

Fortunately, 70 was complete for the bypass of Grand Junction, the only town of any size we came to during the morning. We were running along beside the Colorado River now, through rough tumbling magnificent scenic country, and neither of us cared about it at all.

Not far from Grand Junction we crossed into Utah, and the countryside became wilder and wilder, the towns fewer and smaller and more temporary looking. The landscape was like something from another planet, like movie recreations of Mars; barren chalky cliffs, great gray hills of what looked like ashes, pink and purple stony valleys. It was an unpleasant land, inhospitable, perfectly matching our mood, and we fled through it like Bonnie and Clyde.

Route 70 failed again in the middle of this wasteland, leaving us more of US 6 to contend with, and when signs began to appear warning of a hundred-mile stretch ahead without gas stations we stopped to fill up and Katharine said, "I have to call Barry."

"Yes."

She looked small and forlorn in the phone booth at the edge of the station's blacktop. She was still on the call when I'd finished at the pump, so I drove the cab over and stopped by the booth. After a minute she stuck her head out and said, "Barry wants to talk to you."

"All right," I said.

There was a small fitful breeze and the air was dry, but it was very hot. My T-shirt stuck to me, front and back, and the phone booth was like a sauna. Katharine stood outside it, watching me worriedly, and I said, "Yes?"

"First of all, Thomas," said the voice, "I want to apologize for the way I talked to you last time."

"That's okay," I said. It was okay; we were far beyond that now.

"I can't bring myself to get mad at Katharine," he explained, "and I just took it out on you. I'm sorry."

"Situation understood," I assured him.

"Okay. Thank you. Katharine tells me you're in Utah."

"Right."

"How far do you figure you'll get today?"

"Nevada," I said. "We'll go down Interstate 15, and I'll stop at the first Holiday Inn I see the other side of the Nevada line."

Surprised, he said, "That's a hell of a long distance, isn't it?"

"About six hundred miles. We got an early start today, we're making good time. And that'll give us less than four hundred miles to Los Angeles tomorrow."

"Then I apologize all over again," he said. "Not only shouldn't I have taken my frustration out on you, but you were right and I was wrong. You know your business, Thomas."

"It's Tom," I said.

"Tom? I'm Barry, Tom, and I'm looking forward to shaking your hand."

"Yeah," I said, and then felt impelled to add, "Me, too."

He wanted to talk to Katharine again. I waited in the car, feeling the sweat driblets running down my body beneath my shirt, and when Katharine finished and got back in I started up at once, wanting that breeze. She said, "You told Barry we'd get to Los Angeles tomorrow."

"Right."

"That's good."

"Yes, it is."

I could sense her looking at my profile, but I kept my own eyes facing front. After a minute, very softly she said, "I'm sorry, Tom."

"Hush," I said.

## 41

Westward into increasingly inhuman country. Route 70 re-
appeared, as a two-lane road, a straight lonely line across the
broken landscape, and we ran and ran under the hot dry sun,
past black cliff faces and tortured boulders parodying trees,
where nothing grew.

After Salina there was no Route 70 at all, and our path turned
south along US 89. We found a sun-bleached diner for lunch,
where the customers and waitresses were all uniformly parched
and bitter, made juiceless and ancient by the sun and the hostile terrain. Our hamburgers were small and dry and gray, our
french fries were twisted like torture victims, our coffee was
watery.

During lunch Katharine said, "Tom, I can't stand us not
talking to one another."

"I'm talking to you," I said. "Constantly, in the cab, I'm saying
whole sentences to you, pointing at weird rocks and so on. I'm
just not saying them out loud."

Smiling, she said, "I'm doing the same thing. It's only this
afternoon and tomorrow, could we try actually saying them out
loud to one another?"

"There are things I could say about this hamburger."

"Don't. It may have been someone we know."

Things were somewhat better after that, with casual conversation once more, but it wasn't exactly the same as before. We
were now like those radio call-in shows that put a seven-second
delay between the person on the phone saying something and
the statement actually going out over the air; just in case the

caller has something obscene or libelous or otherwise unacceptable to say. I had a seven-second delay tape working in my head, checking all my statements before releasing them, and from her timing I suspected Katharine had the same. We were almost as we had been, but we were no longer quite live.

By circuitous paths we attained Interstate 15, a highway that rises in Montana at the Canadian border and runs south through Idaho and Utah before angling southwestward through a tiny corridor of Arizona and the bottom of Nevada—including Las Vegas—then crossing the Mojave Desert down into Los Angeles. This was to be our road from now on, and the simple absurd fact that we were traveling *down* the map rather than *across* it made the trip seem somehow easier, faster.

The countryside continued huge and dry and mostly empty, but it was gradually losing that alien quality; we were returning to Terra. The buttes and valleys were now like those in Western movies rather than science-fiction, and here and there were farms and low tundra-like forests. The descending sun today was off to our right, watching us benignly for a change. Katharine and I played Superghost and laughed at one another's jokes.

It was around seven when we left Utah for our thirty-mile slice of Arizona. "These are called the Virgin Mountains," Katharine said, reading yet another roadmap. I looked around at the tumbled striated barren lifeless sandstone all around us; not a soft place anywhere to put your foot, not a flat place to spread your blanket, not a shadow that wasn't the transient shadow of a rock. The road was an undulating ribbon over chasms and gorges, between tall serrated peaks. "They can stay Virgins as far as I'm concerned," I said.

There was one exit in Arizona, where a sign promised a town called Littlefield, but among the sharp boulders I saw only a small corkscrew road climbing painfully away into silence and absence. And ten miles later we attained Nevada, at a town called Mesquite. And crossed from Mountain to Pacific Time; our last lost hour.

"If I'd taken the plane," Katharine said, "the decision would be four days in the past now. I'd be used to it, whatever it was."

"If you'd taken the plane," I said, "I'd be driving around New York now feeling uneasy, thinking I'd missed something and not knowing what it was."

Katharine looked stricken. "Say something funny," she said. "Quick."

"I just did."

## 42

A Holiday Inn restaurant with unshrouded windows! We sat by one, looking out at the tumbling tiny Virgin River while the Muzak doggedly chewed and swallowed *Scatterbrain*: "STILL it's CHAR ming CHAT ter SCAT ter BRAIN."

During the meal Katharine talked about Barry: "We were at dinner once, in Los Angeles, and a girl came over to the table, one of his patients that he hadn't seen for a couple of years. She was very tall and slender, with those great heaps of blonde hair that I envy so much, and she had an absolutely perfect, absolutely blank face. It was just a collection of perfect face parts all put together exactly right, with no lines and no personality and no sense that there was anybody at all *inside* there."

"A store window dummy," I suggested.

"Worse. Store window dummies are hard, the flesh isn't real. This was like a marvelous recreation in lifelike rubberized plastic. And you know what she said?"

"It spoke?"

"It spoke. It said, 'Doctor, you brought out the real me.' "

I laughed, and Katharine pointed at me. "That's right. The only reaction is to laugh. Sitting there at that table, right in front of her when she said it, I still had to smile, and cover my mouth with my hand. But Barry didn't laugh."

"Well, no, he couldn't."

"But he didn't afterward either. He thanked her very solemnly, and told her she was one of his most beautiful creations, and when she left I made some smart-aleck remark—"

"You?"

She grinned. "You might not believe it, Tom, but I can be actually caustic at times. Anyway, I said something or other, and Barry said, 'But she's telling the truth, I *did* bring out the real her. She used to be a very pretty girl,' he said, 'but what she wanted to be was anonymous. She's a frightened empty girl with nothing in her head, but she used to *look* as though she might be interesting in some way. It made her miserable. Now everybody knows she's an empty beautiful creature, and there are people who value her for that, and she's much happier.' He said he counted her among his finest accomplishments."

"Ah hah."

"The point is, he has so much *understanding*. I can be difficult at times, I know I can, and Barry surely knows it, but he never never misunderstands me. He always knows what I mean, even when I'm completely wrongheaded."

"Katharine," I said, "you keep arguing the man's good points, as though that was an issue, but of course it isn't. What's right with Barry was established a long time ago. The question that's left is, what's wrong with you."

She looked very troubled. "Yes, that *is* it, I know it is. But I keep running away from the tough question and answering the easy question all over again. So what *is* wrong with me? Am I afraid of perfection?"

"You've never been afraid of *me*."

"Then that can't be it," she acknowledged. "Come on, Tom, you've see me in inaction for the last five days. What's my problem?"

"Your problem is," I said, "you don't want to marry Mister Right."

"Well, that's succinct." She thought about it, then said, "And it's correct, too. Barry is Mister Right, and that's why I can't bring myself to let him go. But at the same time, I can't bring myself to marry him."

"Why not?"

"I don't know. But I *have* to know by sometime tomorrow. And, Tom," she said, very firmly, "I'll tell you *one* decision I've come to, and I'll stick by it, and that's a promise. And you know me and promises."

"Yes, I do. What's the decision?"

"When I see Barry tomorrow, if I still don't have any *sensible* reason for saying no, I'm going to say yes."

"Ah hah."

"I *want* to say yes anyway, and part of me does understand that all of this is just foolishness, so if this idiot brain inside my head doesn't come up with something pretty compelling by the time we reach Los Angeles, I'm going to make the leap."

"Well," I said, "I have always wanted to be a bridesmaid. How would you and Barry like to take a honeymoon cab ride to New York?"

"That's not funny," she said. And she meant it.

## 43

We were crossing the lobby after dinner, and a tall man in a light blue sports jacket and gray slacks was checking in at the desk. He turned, and Katharine gasped and said, "Oh, my God!" And I knew.

He saw us and walked in our direction, smiling. As he approached, I said quietly to Katharine, "He doesn't look much like his picture."

He was, in fact, more handsome than the picture, and taller than I'd supposed. He was one of those men with a calmly self-confident walk; you knew he would always be modest, and always be capable of dealing with the situation. He came up to us with a happy but slightly apologetic grin on his face, saying, "Katharine, you're just going to have to forgive me. I decided I couldn't wait another day to see you." Turning to me, he extended his hand and his smile and said, "You must be Tom."

"And you absolutely *have* to be Barry."

We exchanged a brief solid handshake and he said, with some amusement, "You aren't exactly what I expected."

"On the other hand, you're precisely what I expected. Katharine has spent the last five days describing your perfections."

He studied me a few seconds, to see if I was pulling his leg, but I wasn't; when he'd reassured himself he said, "Katharine keeps telling *me* how wonderful I am, too. Unfortunately, it's mostly over the long-distance phone. By the way, you *didn't* stop at the first Holiday Inn on the Nevada side."

"The sun was still fairly high," I explained, "and I still felt fresh, so we did some more miles. I had no idea we were meeting."

"Neither did I." Explaining more to Katharine than me, he said, "But after the phone call I started thinking, and I just couldn't wait anymore. So I took a plane to Vegas, and rented a car, and drove on up. I've spent the last hour checking parking lots for a New York cab."

"This isn't fair, Barry," Katharine said. Her voice sounded strained. "I told you I'd make my mind up by Los Angeles, and that won't be until tomorrow."

"I'm not here asking for *answers*, honey," he told her. "I just wanted to be around you, that's all. If you'd like to talk anything over with me, I'm here and I'm available. If not, that's up to you, and I guarantee you right now I won't press for an answer until we're actually in Westwood."

"Barry," she said, "tell me the truth. Do you have it in the back of your mind, here we are in Nevada anyway, we could get married right now and not have to go through the whole round trip, all the way to Los Angeles and then back here and then back there again?"

"Definitely not," he said. "I'll tell you what I *do* have in mind, though. The plane I chartered this afternoon; I talked to the pilot, and he could fly us to Vegas the day after tomorrow and then fly us right back to Los Angeles again." Grinning, he said, "You won't mind a plane ride *after* you make your decision, will you?"

"I don't want to think about the day after tomorrow," she said. "I want to think about tomorrow and that's all." She was upset, but I knew she'd been *going* to be upset anyway, the next day; this merely moved the crisis forward twenty-four hours. On the other hand, while I understood Barry's anxiousness, it seemed to me he'd made a mistake. If it was possible for him to drive her away, it would be by pushing too hard.

He himself sensed that, I guess; at least he downplayed the

meaning of his presence here, saying, "We'll take it one day at a time, honey, and that's a promise. Anyway, I have to finish checking in. I'm in room two twenty-six if you feel like phoning later." To me he gave another brief smile and nod, saying, "Nice to meet you."

"And you."

I watched him return to the desk, where the clerk was waiting for his signature. When I looked at Katharine, she was gazing at his back with a very tortured expression. "He won't press," I assured her. "He's just over-anxious, that's all."

"Good night, Tom," she said, not looking at me, but at Barry's back. "I'll see you in the morning."

"Sure," I said, and went away. Looking back across the lobby from the doorway, I saw them both still in the same positions; but soon the clerk would release Barry and he would turn around. I went on to my room.

# 44

What is she going to do?

The unread saga sat atop the TV in my inevitably identical room—the curtain was green in the proxy-Utrillo on the left—but I neither read nor watched, having no patience for anything other than my own troubled feelings. I paced the thick-carpeted floor, asking myself pointless questions and giving myself very few satisfactory answers.

What is she going to do? What *is* she going to do?

Well, what do I want her to do?

I want her to find happiness and contentment. I want her to be sure of herself. I want her to get unstuck before she comes unglued.

What do I think she *should* do? I think – though an inane part of me resists this – I think she should marry Barry. He's strong, and he's wise, and he'll leave her sufficient space around herself, and she'll work out her problems much better after she's made her decision and knows for sure which set of problems she'll be dealing with. Unless, of course, she finds herself shrinking next to his great size, which is always a possibility, particularly with women, and which may be one of the unconscious fears she has about him. In which case, she will either get out of the marriage eventually, in some messy or relatively civilized way, or she will crumble like an old adobe wall and become a beige mound where a person had once stood.

And if I were to take her away from all this, on my yellow charger, as the romantic ten-year-old inside me keeps suggesting, *where* would I take her? And how? And for how long?

And would she want to go? *I'm* not going to ask her to marry me, any more than I'm going to get another job as an executive trainee. I'm who I am, and if I struggle myself into some other posture it can only be for a little while; sooner or later I'll be forced to relax into who I really am—which is what happened to me in the past—so what's the point pretending? Katharine and I have worked it out that we can get along very well on a non-sexual basis for five days while riding together in an automobile, but that's not quite enough to go on with, even if Barry didn't already exist, which he does. Barry loves her, Barry wants to marry her, Barry really and truly is the perfect guy for her. And she loves Barry, she told me so herself several times in the last few days. I am merely another distraction from the insistent unanswered question.

What *is* she going to do?

Whose room are they in right now? Are they together? Will they sleep together? Her room or his room?

How did I get myself into this thing? No matter how it ends for her, it can only end miserably for me. I'd have been better off if she'd flagged some other cab last Thursday. Any other cab.

And so would she.

Yeah, that's the truth. I didn't help simplify her problem, I complicated it by introducing an irrelevant Other Man.

I thought of Rita for the first time since I'd left her that note about the yogurt back in New York. Rita's answered Katharine's question, hasn't she? At least for the moment. She's answered it in the same way I have, by limiting the dosage to a non-lethal quantity.

And Sue Ann, too.

Katharine wants to know how much a non-lethal dosage can be. Katharine wants to know if she can walk through the flame and survive. Katharine, if I may be forgiven what sounds like but is not an overstatement, has not given up hope.

What is she going to do? Marriage with Barry will be a vote for hope. So that's another reason why she ought to do it, because Katharine is one of the people for whom hope is a good thing. And because Katharine still does believe in hope, I think she is going to decide in favor of marriage, which is the decision I think she should make, so this conclusion will please me. Won't it?

I sat on the side of the bed and dialed my own phone number in the city—there would be some obscure pleasure or satisfaction if Rita was there, sleeping alone in my bed—and listened to the phone ring and ring in the obviously empty apartment. It was three hours later there, one in the morning, and in my mind I could see the dark rooms, the furniture, the walls, the cubical spaces filled with the spasms of telephone bell. I could call Rita at her own apartment, of course, but it wasn't Rita I wanted, it was the reminder of Rita as having a connection with *me*. I counted forty rings, enjoying the power to have an effect in that place so far away, and when it occurred to me I was probably driving the neighbors right out of their minds I hung up and was alone again.

Around midnight I went out for a drive, pushing my alien cab up dark broad western streets, where mostly the traffic lights played out their patterns just for me. There was no Sue Ann, no Mr. and Mrs. Chasen, no pregnant woman, no CB maniac; there were no adventures. In every life, however reluctantly, you move at last beyond adventure.

# 45

Katharine was alone at the table, having breakfast. Joining her, I said, "Where's Barry?"

"Haven't seen him. He'll be around, no doubt." She didn't sound particularly pleased.

The waitress had met me with a coffeepot. She filled my cup, gave me a menu, and went away. I said, "Didn't you talk things over with him last night?"

"No. We talked for a minute in the lobby, that's all. Mostly about you."

"He isn't jealous," I said. "He's hipper than that."

"No, he isn't jealous. He doesn't think you're trying to take his place. He just thought he could take yours."

"Say again?"

"He thought you should turn around this morning and head east, while I'd drive on to Los Angeles with him in his rented car."

I hated that idea. I said, "What did you tell him?"

"That the cab was where I was doing my thinking, and that I intended to stay in the cab until Los Angeles, and *then* I'd come out and make my decision."

"Good for you."

"But he made me promise," she said, "to talk it over with you. After all, it could save you something like eight hundred miles if you turned around now."

The waitress had come back, pencil poised. "Katharine," I said, "if nothing else, I've got to be around for the finish."

She smiled and said, "Good."

I told the waitress, "Number three, please, over easy. Grapefruit juice."

Katharine said, "There's something else, though. I was thinking about it, last night and this morning, and I *should* talk with Barry before I say yes or no. Before we reach Los Angeles."

Which sounded like a reversal of what she'd just said. "So?"

"You can see it makes sense to discuss it with him, can't you?"

"Sure. But I don't get the point."

"I want him to ride along in the cab."

Immediately I said, "I can't pick up fares outside the five boroughs."

"Please, Tom, be serious with me."

Did she think I wasn't being serious? I said, "What about his rental car?"

"He can turn it in. Tom, it's the right place for the discussion, in the back of that cab. You know it is. It's my turf."

"If only he'd stayed in— Where's he live?"

"Westwood."

"Sounds tacky."

"It isn't," she said, with a little smile. "It's Bel Air, really, but south of Sunset Boulevard. Nor far from UCLA. I redid the grounds."

"Here he comes," I said, looking around the waitress, who was delivering my breakfast.

"Tom, say it's all right."

"It's all right," I lied. The waitress went away, Barry arrived, I got to my feet and we shared another good handshake, a few conventional words were spoken, we all sat down, and I filled my mouth with ham and eggs while Katharine made the suggestion: "Barry, ride to Los Angeles with me."

He was delighted, of course, but cautious, saying, "Are you sure?"

"We'll talk. I think it's a good idea."

"But why make Tom drive all those extra miles, when I've got my own car?"

"No," she said. "You'd be distracted by driving. And it would be *your* car. In the cab, we can just concentrate on the subject."

Barry gave the waitress his order and drank some of the coffee she'd poured him. Then he said, "Katharine, I'm delighted."

"Good," she said. She glanced over at me and I stuffed some toast in my mouth.

# 46

It was about seventy miles to Las Vegas, where Barry could turn in his car. He led the way down Interstate 15, with Katharine and me in the cab behind him. Katharine sat in back, but on the jump seat so we could talk. She kept telling me how unfair she'd been to Barry. "You can see how he is," she said. "You can see I've been very wrong to him."

"If you love him you marry him," I said. "If you don't love him, leave him alone."

"I do love him," she said. "That isn't the question, it really isn't."

I let my silence answer for me.

Las Vegas is from some schlock version of *The Wizard of Oz*. You know, the Emerald City rising up out of the desert. But this is the Ormolu City, plastic towers rising out of the hot dry sand into the hot dry air, fool's gold glittering in the clear empty sunshine sharply enough to make you squint behind your sunglasses. Driving in from the northwest, along an endless flat ironing-board desert landscape, you see it ahead of you like some anti-mirage, which for a long time refuses to get any closer, then is suddenly *there*, held within an acne ring of shacks and sheds and derelict huts.

In the city the streets are wide, the houses in the residential areas seeming lower to the ground than usual, as though all those one-story ranches are sinking inch by inch, year by year, back into the sand. The famous Strip is anxious glitter, clutching your sleeve for attention; a full year's television viewing concentrated into one frantic image, overloaded, overlit, and overexposed. If architecture is frozen music, Las Vegas is an album of polka favorites, frozen too late.

The five minutes the cab spent parked on the treeless shade-less blacktop near the car rental office were enough to bake its interior like the inside of a shepherd's pie. The air was so dry that the sweat evaporated from me almost as rapidly as it oozed to the surface, making my skin feel itchy and dirty. My left arm was in direct sunlight no matter where I put it, and though I was already moderately tanned I could feel the burn.

When Barry got into the cab—Katharine had already trans-ferred to the rear seat—he said, "Wow. You should have gotten one with air-conditioning."

I glanced in the mirror, but Katharine was absorbed in opening her attaché case, as though she hadn't heard him. I started the engine and slid out amid the traffic; long low fat cars that would have looked perfect with a cigar clenched in the teeth of their grills. The sun was so bright you couldn't tell if the traffic lights were red or green; it created a certain amount of suspense as I picked my way back toward Interstate 15.

In back, Katharine was being brisk and businesslike, her lap full of pads of yellow paper. "I've done an awful lot of thinking the past week," she said, "and I wrote some of it down. You can see what you're thinking sometimes if you put it down on paper."

"I know," he said. "I do that myself."

"I think the best thing," she told him, "is for you to read at least part of what I wrote."

"Fine," he said. "Fine."

Route 15. Los Angeles, said the sign, 284 miles.

## 47

Now at last we were in a normal cabby–passenger relationship.
I sat up front and drove, and they sat in back and argued. He
would read a few pages of what she'd written, while she either
watched his face or read over his shoulder, and he would stop
from time to time to disagree with a part of it, or make a comment, or tell her she had misunderstood something. Then they
would discuss it.

They were both very tense, and it seemed to me it would be
good for everybody concerned if they'd yell at one another for a
while, but they both kept very tight control. Katharine was stiff-
lipped and grim, with strain lines over her eyebrows and around
her mouth, while Barry determinedly maintained an easygoing
calm façade. Looking at him in the mirror, it occurred to me to
wonder if *his* face had been altered. Not by himself, obviously,
but perhaps by some other plastic surgeon. Psychiatrists before
they can practice are required to go through psychiatric sessions
with another psychiatrist, so maybe plastic surgeons have to be
made pretty before they can hang out the old shingle. Barry had
an outdoor handsomeness, a pleasing unobtrusive western crag-
giness in a face that was not too deeply tanned. Was it real? If a
fake, it was beautifully done; like Katharine's eight miles of road.

I remembered Katharine's story about the blank-faced girl:
"You brought out the real me." Was that the real Barry back
there, being so patient and calm, like a very good deep-sea fish-
erman giving Katharine all the slack she wanted? Enough rope.
He probably *was* real, and had learned patience with his patients.
Or possibly his calm non-assertive careful capable personality

had come first, and had led him to a career where such characteristics were valuable. And to a woman with whom he could make full use of the same traits.

And then I thought: *He* shouldn't marry *her*. This didn't alter my conviction that it was the right thing for Katharine to marry Barry, that he was the perfect man for her and his presence in her life would calm and soothe her so totally that if I were to see her again in five years I'd barely recognize her; but for Barry, it would be a mistake.

Stupid, of course, but very human; the wrong one had the doubts. She thought marriage with Barry would create problems, whereas it would end all her problems. And he thought his problems would cease if he got her to marry him, but they wouldn't; in fact they would very slightly intensify, as his sense of responsibility formed a cocoon around her. There would be no respite from perfection in his life, not at work and not at home. Some day one of those blank-faced girls would attract his compassion and strength, and he would find the joy of taking care of someone who doesn't really need anyone's concern; the kind of pleasure all cat-lovers know. Calmness, restraint, assurance, strength; he could lavish these on the blank-faced girl with a free hand, secure in the knowledge that she would survive if his attention ever strayed, that he could play at being responsible for her because in fact he couldn't possibly be responsible for her. The duplicity would finally make him miserable, of course, but it wasn't his happiness that concerned me, it was Katharine's. *She* would remain his true responsibility, and so he would make absolutely sure she never never never found out about the blank-faced girl. I thought I could trust him to do that.

So even in perfection there's imperfection. But Katharine would come closer than most people; closer by light-years than

Lynn and I had ever achieved. Driving out across the charred desert while they argued it out behind me, I finally myself grew calm about Katharine. I had become involved in her life the way you get involved in somebody else's chess match, until you almost come to think of yourself as a participant; but now we were in the endgame, we were nearing mate, and my status as mere observer was forcing itself on my attention. I was fond of Katharine, and with calmness I could now approve the happy ending I visualized for her.

The desert also forced itself on my attention as I drove along. At Barry's suggestion, we had prepared ourselves as though this were a serious major desert, and in fact that's exactly what it was. On the seat beside me was a paper bag of super-market fruit, while on the floor in skimpy shade were two gray-white plastic gallon jugs of water.

This desert, called Mojave, had been not so much tamed as beguiled by this baking desert-colored road running straight across the empty miles. Tumbled mountains ringed us, and the road slowly rose and fell, as though we were traveling across fossilized waves from some Paleolithic tempest. Police heli-copters fluttered and flapped above us, watching for motorists who, unwary or unlucky, had broken down. The temperature out here was over a hundred, and the humidity so low that I drove with a peachpit in my mouth to encourage salivation. On this griddle it was easy for automobiles to boil over, to suffer mechanical malfunctions, to abandon hope and die. There were no towns, there was no water, there was only this tightrope wire suspended in the dusty void between Las Vegas and Los Angeles. Between the vultures and the angels.

With police cars patrolling the road and police helicopters floating overhead, I couldn't travel at my usual high speeds but kept myself firmly under sixty from the time we crossed the state line into California. It was more than two hours after we left Las Vegas before we reached the next settlement of man, a town called Barstow, a small bleached stucco outpost of diners and junkyards in the desert, where I took the exit and found a McDonald's. Barry treated, and we ate on the move, needing the breeze of our motion to keep us from roasting in this hot-crock cab.

Now the road turned southerly, toward Victorville and San Bernardino and Pasadena, and the couple in the back seat ate their Big Macs and drank their Cokes and took a rest from their discussion. Traffic had been thin all across the Mojave, as though we had been part of an old camel caravan trail on the Sahara, but south of Barstow there were more cars and a returning sense that life was after all possible on this planet. More optimistically Barry and Katharine began to talk again:

"I know it sounds stupid," she said, "but what I wrote there is true. I'm afraid of demanding too much from you, that my need for independence will itself be a heavy dependency on you, weighing you down." (Close to what I had been thinking myself, across the desert. Would he understand the hint, would he see the danger?)

No. "Your independence is one of the things I most treasure about you," he said, fatuously earnest. "That's why I wouldn't think of trying to change it, and why it couldn't possibly hurt me in any way. You must have your own space, your own feelings, your own privacies and selfhood. I've always respected that, and of *course* I'll go on respecting it after we're married."

Of course he would, but what he didn't understand was that after the marriage the strain on him would be so much greater that it would weigh him down; precisely as Katharine had said. But she didn't fully understand it either, and was only groping for what troubled her in the darkness of the future, so her answer was merely more words, reiterating without explaining.

And that was the way they went, all day long, four hours of it in the cab as we crossed the desert and descended into the spreading exurbia of Los Angeles. They repeated the same arguments in different words, combined old thoughts in new ways, circled around and around the black dense contra-terrine boulder of Katharine's doubt. And we came at last to the top of a long descent down a naked mountain slope, ten miles of sweeping broad roadway leading from the barren plateau into— the nether world. The entrance to Los Angeles. Yellow-gray smog covered the valley in a thick cloud, like a dirty smoke-screen. Cars far ahead disappeared gradually down into it, while in the northbound lanes other tiny cars, apparently unharmed, emerged from that unmoving yeast at the bottom of the bowl and scampered up the long slope toward sunlight.

We slid down and down, and as we neared the smog it seemed for a while very slightly to recede; but we overtook it, and plunged in, and from the back seat Katharine, surprised out of her argument, cried out, "My God! What's happened? A forest fire?"

The sky down here on the valley floor was gray, the sun a dime-size white circle with a red rim, the air yellow-tinged. Greenery flanked the roadway, amazingly enough, and here at the bottom were houses, neighborhoods, children on skate-boards breathing and living.

They wonder if man can adapt to other planets. He already has.

Barry said, "It's smog. This part gets the worst of it, the wind brings it all east to the mountains. We usually don't have any smog at all in Westwood."

Katharine laughed—for the first time today—and said, "Barry, I'm not going to decide yes or no on the basis of smog!"

## 48

The San Bernardino Freeway, westbound. We went through Ontario, Pomona, West Covina, El Monte, Rosemead, Alhambra. Barry was right, the smog did lessen the farther west we traveled, but it never entirely disappeared. By the time we reached the city line of Los Angeles proper, it was merely a metallic glitter in the air, a sharp taste in the back of the throat, a faint burning at the corners of the eyes.

The discussion in back had worn itself down to a smooth eroded artifact, a kind of separate third presence back there, slowly fading into a ghost; to haunt them? Barry broke a long silence to call, "Tom, take the Golden State Freeway south."

"Right."

"But then stay to the right; you'll be taking the Santa Monica Freeway next."

"Okay."

In a quieter, almost pitying voice he said, "Katharine, we're nearly there."

"I know." She sounded tired, prepared to say yes just to end it; game called because of weariness. The right answer, but for the wrong reason.

There was heavy traffic now, four lanes of it in each direction. I wanted so much to keep my eyes on the mirror, but I couldn't. My attention was divided as we negotiated the Golden State and then the Santa Monica Freeways, the cab weaving and wobbling through all those purposeful Mercedes-Benzes and Volkswagens. Santa Monica Freeway; less than fifteen miles to go.

We'd done five of them before Barry spoke again: "Katharine, we've talked it out. We've discussed it many times in the past, but this time we've exhausted it, haven't we?"

"Yes." They'd exhausted *her*.

"There's nothing left to say."

In the mirror, she silently shook her head.

"Katharine," he said, gentle but insistent, "is there any *reason* why it would be wrong for you to marry me?"

She didn't answer for a long time, but he let her go, he didn't repeat the question, he merely waited. He would be very good for her.

"No."

"Katharine, you know I love you."

"Barry, I've never doubted that for a second."

"Do you love me?"

"Oh, *yes*, Barry, that's one of the few things I'm sure of."

"Tom," he called, "take the San Diego Freeway north, get off at Wilshire Boulevard."

"Right."

"Katharine, we're nearly home."

"I know."

"Katharine. Will you marry me?"

Her face was drained. There *was* a mistake here somewhere! I wanted to shout something, but there weren't any words.

"Yes," she said.

I couldn't help what happened to the cab, or what lanes it wandered through; all my attention was riveted to that mirror. Barry was looking thunderstruck, but delight was emerging, like the sun coming through rainclouds. Katharine was smiling at him, shaky but relieved, the strain lines already fading from her face.

"Katharine, yes? *Now?*"

"We'll take that plane this afternoon."

Honking all around me. I didn't want to look in the mirror anymore anyway; let them embrace in private. I got the cab back on an even keel, ignored all those drivers behind glass silently shouting at me in their air-conditioned isolation, and just ahead saw the exit for Wilshire Boulevard.

Barry had come up for air: "Turn right," he called, "and take the fourth left."

"Right."

There was a traffic light at the end of the exit ramp. I stopped, then made my turn and began counting blocks. At *one* was a red light; I stopped. My eyes were determinedly forward.

Behind me, Barry was reassuring her: "Sweetheart, you won't be sorry. You know how much I cherish you, I'll make everything possible for you."

"I know you will."

"Now that you're going to be mine, we can—"

"Yours?"

"What?"

Katharine said, "I'm going to be *yours*?"

There was something new in her voice, some completely strange and different note. And *now* the damn light turned green. I drove forward, in city traffic, with pedestrians everywhere.

Behind me Barry, sounding bewildered but also anxious, said, "Of course you'll be mine. You'll be my wife."

"You'll *own* me?"

"It's not owning," he said. "And besides, I'll be yours, too. If I'll own you, then you'll own me."

"But I don't want to own you. I don't want to own anybody."

"It's just a phrase, Katharine. 'Be mine.' It means be my love."

"Be my Valentine," she said, in a thoughtful way. "Let me make you mine."

"Those are just *phrases*."

"No, they're not. They say what they mean. 'Let me *make* you mine.' If we marry each other. We have proprietary rights."

"Oh, Katharine, not all over again. Not *again*."

"Thank goodness you said that. Now I finally know what was wrong."

Was this the fourth block? How am I supposed to count to four under such conditions? Screw it; I turned left.

"Katharine, I thought we were through with all— Tom? Tom, where are we? *This* isn't the right street!"

"I counted to four. I *thought* I counted to four."

"Pull over, Tom," he said, sounding harried. "Park for a while, I can't— I'm sorry, I can't think about directions right now."

"Okay with me," I said. It was fine with me. In fact, at last everything was fine with me. There was a parking space on the right, just before a restaurant called Lancaster Abbey, made up to look like a medieval stone monastery; I pulled in there, cut the engine, and settled down to pretend I wasn't looking in the mirror.

Katharine was no longer weary; eagerly she was explaining things to Barry, who watched her as though she had suddenly without warning right in front of him turned into a frog. "What threw me off," she was saying, "was that you were Mister Right. I knew there was something wrong, but I didn't know what it was. I thought maybe there was something the matter with you and I just wasn't seeing it. Or I thought there was something the matter with *me*, but *you* couldn't see it."

"Katharine, you're not making sense."

Yes, she was. She said, "What was wrong all along was *marriage*.

People have asked me to marry them before, Tom asked me about that, and— Tom?"

I looked around, an innocent bystander. "Mm?"

Barry was having a hell of a time keeping up. "*Tom* asked you to marry him?"

"Of course not," she said. "He asked me if I hadn't been proposed to before. And I was, Tom, and I told you about one of them."

"The Tupperware boy."

"That's right. And he was obviously wrong, so when I said no I thought I was saying no to *him*."

"Ah hah," I said. "I see the point."

"Well, I'll be damned if *I* see the point," Barry said. He was finally getting bugged, but was remaining a gentleman about it.

Katharine told him, "The thing I couldn't get hold of was, the problem wasn't in *you* and it wasn't in *me*, it was in *marriage*. I don't want to get married. It's as simple as that."

"You don't want to get married."

"But I never knew it. I always thought, well, I don't want to marry *him* because he has this wrong with him, and I don't want to marry *him* because he has that wrong with him, and when I met you and you didn't have anything wrong with you I was just stymied. I couldn't bring myself to marry you, and honest to *God*, Barry, I just simply didn't know why."

"You don't want to get married." He kept repeating that as though it were a simple absurdity, and if he just said it often enough Katharine would recognize it as an absurdity and they could go on to talk about something else. The wedding, for instance.

But all Katharine did was repeat it back to him: "That's right, I don't want to get married. But you do, Barry, and I respect that. Maybe someday I will, too, though to tell the truth I really doubt it. What we've had the last two years is all I have to offer."

"The last two years have driven me crazy," he said, very quietly.

"I know. I'm sorry. I'm wrong for you."

They were both silent a while. I blatantly remained half turned in their direction, gawping at them directly rather than through the mirror, but neither seemed aware of my presence. Katharine gazed at Barry with tenderness and concern—and relief—and Barry studied her face, his own hands and knees, the sidewalk, the passing traffic, even the notice at the back of my headrest: Ask Driver For Out Of Town Rates. And finally, head down, eyes watching his fingers tap together between his knees, he said, "I can't do it anymore, Katharine."

"I know you can't."

"It isn't that I won't ask you again. It's that I *can't* ask again."

"I know that, too. But if you did ask again, I finally know what the answer would be."

He turned his head at that and looked at her, for a long silent time. Then he nodded slightly, saying, "Yes, I see."

"I'm sorry I was so stupid for so long," she said.

"No." A kind of ironic bitterness came into his voice, and he said, "You were hard to *get*. Hard to *catch*. You weren't easy to *capture*, and I was determined to *make you mine*. I guess I do know what you're talking about, though I don't agree with the conclusion. And I do love you." He touched her cheek with the tips of his fingers. "Goodbye."

"Barry." Which was her form of goodbye.

He opened his door, then gave me a little half-amused smile. "Nice to meet you, Tom."

"And you."

He got out of the car and walked away, back toward Wilshire.

I looked at Katharine and she said to me, "I'm right. I'm finally right."

"I believe you are. And what would you like to do next?"

She glanced around. "Would that restaurant have a bar, do you suppose?"

"It very well might," I said.

## 49

It did. The bar was tricked up to look like a monastery's wine cellar, but fortunately the only light in the joint came from stubby candles on the tables, so we couldn't see most of the décor. Katharine had used up her decision-making powers for today, and couldn't even think about what sort of drink she might want, so I ordered Bloody Marys for two. "It's food," I explained to her, and when they arrived they were even more food than I'd anticipated; being California Bloody Marys, they'd arrived complete with a long stalk of celery each, for a swizzle stick.

We munched and drank in companionable silence for a while and then I said, "What do you do now?"

She shrugged; she wasn't anxious about anything anymore. "Go back to New York. Get caught up on that *pile* of work waiting for me. Live my life."

"Can I ask you a question?"

"Sure."

"Just as a point of information," I said, "would you consider marrying *me*?"

She stared at me. "You?"

"Just a hypothetical question," I assured her.

"Now, don't *you* start," she said, pointing her celery at me. "Barry was Mister Right, and if I said no to him, why would I say yes to *you*? You're the worst offer I've had since the Tupperware boy."

"Aw, I'm not *that* bad."

"At least he was going to graduate school."

"Anyway," I said, "it was just to get it straight, clear the air, have no misunderstandings, give us something to go forward from. I tell you what, I'll quit the cab, I'll be your chauffeur."

"I don't need a car in New York," she said.

"Oh. Okay. Then I'll be your younger brother."

She stared at me in the candlelight. "What do you mean, brother? What do you mean, *younger*?"

"I want to hang out with you," I explained. "I'm just trying to work out the relationship."

"We can discuss it," she said, "on the way back."

The discussion continues.

# AFTERWORD

The story goes that Donald Westlake once wrestled with the question, *What would a caper novel be without any crime in it?* The result was his novel *Brothers Keepers*, about a group of monks in New York City fighting to keep their centuries-old monastery from being demolished to make room for a high-rise. It's a wonderful novel and we reprinted it in Hard Case Crime a couple of years back. There's a tiny bit of crime in the book, but only a tiny bit: a stolen lease, a fire set to cover the thief's tracks, a punch or two thrown that might count as assault if you squint. Don was originally planning to title the book *The Felonious Monks*, which is a great title, but he couldn't, because the monks in the story turned out not to be felonious. Sometimes that's what happens. Your characters surprise you, and if you're a great writer, you go with it, you let them lead the way. From an email Don wrote to a friend: "I have to tell you a teeny thing about the genesis of *Brothers Keepers*...I started it and introduced the [monks] and realized I liked them too much to lead them into a life of crime. So, to begin with, there went the title. 'Okay,' I said, 'let's see what a caper novel looks like without the caper.' Turned out to be a love story; who knew."

Also turns out that wasn't Don's first experiment along these lines.

Who knows what story he thought he was going to tell when he first got Katharine Scott into Tom Fletcher's taxi one day in the late 1970s. Maybe he thought they'd encounter gangsters or bank robbers on their journey west to Los Angeles; maybe he was imagining a Bonnie-and-Clyde crime spree. But what happened instead was, they fell in love. Who knew?

So: there's no crime in this book. (That one speeding incident hardly counts. Even if the police put in a cameo appearance.) But just as *Brothers Keepers* is a caper novel in spite of its minimal criminal content, this one is a suspense novel through and through. Don, ever the ingenious experimenter with form, found an answer to the question, *Can you have a suspense novel without any crime in it?* And the answer is a resounding yes. We're on the edge of our seats the whole ride, as the miles tick down and Katharine's moment of decision comes into focus. Will she or won't she? What will she decide and *how* will she decide, and will these two kids, who clearly deserve happiness and deserve each other, manage to not get torn apart by the inexorable pull of matrimony and respectability and doing what's expected?

Don's first stab at *Call Me a Cab* was 215 pages long in typescript and ended pretty much the way you just read, but it started differently:

> *This isn't my story. The actual hero of this story is a twenty-nine year old terrific woman named Katharine Scott. I was just along for the ride.*

Ironically, opening with the narrator saying it's not his story put the focus more on him than if he'd just shut up and let Katharine take center stage from the start. So somewhere along the way, on a subsequent trip the manuscript took through his typewriter, Don made that change. He also added something like 50 more pages to the book. The entire sequence where the cab breaks down and Tom and Katharine meet the Chasens—some of the very best stuff in the book—wasn't in the book to begin with.

It also wasn't in the abridged novelette-length version of the book that ran as a feature in *Redbook* magazine, which is the only place any portion of this book has ever appeared before. But a lot of things were missing from the *Redbook* version. Every few pages lost a paragraph or two, every few paragraphs lost a sentence or two, every few sentences lost a word or two—it's what happens when you compress a book down into a magazine piece. Still, Tom and Katharine had their debut, even if abridged too far, and you'd think their full-length adventure would have followed. But no. The manuscript sat on a shelf for the next four decades, waiting for someone to give it a chance.

Part of the reason may have been that in his later revisions Don experimented with alternate paths to the destination: in one draft, he had Katharine and Tom fall into bed together at the Hilyerds and wake up regretting it. It may have been a consummation devoutly to be wished, but it changed the book's climax (you'll pardon the expression) in ways that weren't entirely satisfying. He also experimented with Barry not making an appearance in the book at all—we drive all the way to L.A., but the book ends outside Barry's house, without the man showing his handsome face and without giving Katharine the opportunity to speak her piece to him.

This version—the version you just read—incorporates the best elements from each draft, and I want to thank Abby Westlake and Stephen Moore (one of Don's agents of long standing) for turning up all the manuscripts and other materials they were able to provide. Editing unpublished work from an author who's no longer with us is always a challenge, requiring humility and care. I feel fortunate to have had years to work with Don and learn about his preferences when it came to editorial matters, not to mention the privilege of editing three previous unpublished novels of his (*Memory*, *The Comedy is Finished*, and *Forever and a Death*—every one of them a great read). I hope you'll agree that this last lost book of Don's—and I do think it's the last one, though I've been wrong about that before—is a wonderful final gift from an author we all love and miss so much.

For a child of the 1970s like yours truly, the book is a glorious time capsule full of things that no longer exist, starting with payphones and Checker cabs. For a novel of its time, it's a refreshingly strong feminist portrayal of a determined woman taking control of her life and making her own choices. It's also the only book I know that contains *literal* borscht-belt comedy. ("His clothing was still all burgundy and white, with white patent leather shoes. As we went by, I leaned down and said to him, 'You wear that outfit in the Belmore Cafeteria, they'll think you're the soup of the day.'")

And if you're wondering what the book is doing in a line called Hard Case Crime when it's got no crime in it, my answer is, sometimes you have to allow yourself to travel off the beaten path and follow the road where it leads you. A change of scenery can do a world of good. And seeing as how it's February as we're publishing this, perhaps love was on our minds.

After all, though they may revoke my *noir* editor credentials for saying this, Saint Valentine's Day is not *only* for massacres.

Charles Ardai
February 2022

# WANT MORE
# WESTLAKE?

### If you enjoyed
## CALL ME A CAB,
### you'll love

# BROTHERS
# KEEPERS

### available now from your favorite
### local or online bookseller.

### Read on for a sample...

# One

"Bless me. Father, for I have sinned. It has been four days since my last confession."

"Yes, yes. Go on."

Why does he always sound so impatient? Rush rush rush; that's not the proper attitude. "Well," I said, "let's see." I tried not to be rattled. "I had an impure thought," I said, "on Thursday evening, during a shaving commercial on television."

"A shaving commercial?" Now he sounded exasperated; it was bad enough, apparently, that I bored him, without bewildering him as well.

"It's a commercial," I said, "in which a blonde lady with a Swedish accent applies shaving cream to the face of a young man with a rather prognathous jaw."

"Prognathous?" More bewildered than exasperated this time; I'd caught his attention for fair.

"That means, uh, prominent. A large jaw, that sort of sticks out."

"Does that have anything to do with the sin?"

"No, no. I just thought, uh, I thought you wanted to know, uh…"

"This impure thought," he said, chopping off my unfinished sentence. "Did it concern the woman or the man?"

"The woman, of course! What do you think?" I was shocked; you don't expect to hear that sort of thing in confession.

"All right," he said. "Anything else?" His name is Father Banzolini, and he comes here twice a week to hear our confessions.

We give him a nice dinner before and a nightcap after, but he's surly all the time, a very surly priest. I imagine he finds us dull, and would rather be hearing confessions over in the theater district or down in Greenwich Village. After all, how far can a lamb stray in a monastery?

"Um," I said, trying to think. I'd had all my sins organized in my mind before coming in here, but as usual Father Banzolini's asperity had thrown me off course. I'd once thought I might jot down all my sins in advance and simply read them from the paper in the confessional, but somehow that lacked the proper tone for contrition and so on. Also, what if the paper were to fall into the wrong hands?

Father Banzolini cleared his throat.

"Um," I said hurriedly. "I, uh, I stole an orange Flair pen from Brother Valerian."

"You *stole* it? Or you borrowed it?"

"I stole it," I said, somewhat proudly. "On purpose."

"Why?"

"Because he did the puzzle in last Sunday's *Times*, and he knows that's my prerogative. He claims he forgot. I imagine you'll be hearing the story from his side a little later tonight."

"Never mind anyone else's sins," Father Banzolini said. "Did you make restitution?"

"Beg pardon?"

A long artificial sigh. "Did you give it back?"

"No, I lost it. You didn't see it, did you? It's an ordinary orange—"

"No, I did not see it!"

"Oh. Well, I know it's around here somewhere, and when I find it I'll give it right back."

"Good," he said. "Of course, if you don't find it you'll have to replace it."

Forty-nine cents. I sighed, but said, "Yes, I know, I will."

"Anything else?"

I wished I could say no, but it seemed to me there had been something more than the Flair pen and the impure thought. Now, what was it? I cast my mind back.

"Brother Benedict?"

"I'm thinking," I said. "Yes!"

He gave a sudden little jump, the other side of the small screened window. "Sorry," I said. "I didn't mean to startle you. But I remember the other one."

"There's more," he said, without joy.

"Just one. I took the Lord's name in vain."

He rested his chin on his hand. It was hard to see his face in the semidark, but his eyes appeared hooded, perhaps entirely closed. "Tell me about it," he said.

"I was in the courtyard," I told him, "and Brother Jerome was washing windows on the second floor when he dropped the cloth. It landed on my head, wet and cold and utterly without warning, and I instinctively shouted, *'Jesus Christ!'* "

He jumped again.

"Whoops," I whispered. "Did I say that too loud?"

He coughed a bit. "Perhaps more than was absolutely necessary," he said. "Is *that* all of it?"

"Yes," I said. "Definitely."

"And do you have contrition and a firm purpose of amendment?"

"Oh, positively," I said.

"Good." He roused himself a bit, lifting his chin from his propped hand and shifting around on his chair. "For your penance, say two Our Fathers and, oh, seven Hail Marys."

That seemed a bit steep for three little sins, but penances are non-negotiable. "Yes, Father," I said.

"And it might be a good idea to close your eyes during television commercials."

"Yes, Father."

"Now say a good act of contrition."

I closed my eyes and said the prayer, hearing him mumble the absolution in slurred Latin at the same time, and then my turn was finished and I left the confessional, my place being taken at once by old Brother Zebulon, tiny, bent, wrinkled and white-haired. He nodded at me and slipped behind the curtain, out of sight but not out of hearing; the cracking of his joints as he knelt down in there sounded through the chapel like a pair of rifle shots.

I knelt at the altar rail to zip through my penance, all the time trying to think where that blasted Flair could be. I'd taken it Thursday afternoon, and when I'd changed my mind the next morning—felt remorseful, in fact—the pen was absolutely nowhere to be found. This was Saturday night, and I had now spent the last day and a half looking for it, with so far not the slightest trace. What on earth had I done with it?

Finishing my penance without having solved the mystery of the missing Flair, I left the chapel and looked at the big clock in the hall. Ten-forty. The Sunday *Times* would be at the newsstand by now. I hurried along toward the office to get the necessary sixty cents and official permission to leave the premises.

Brother Leo was on duty at the desk, reading one of his aviation magazines. He was the exception to the rule. Brother Leo, an extremely stout man who wasn't the slightest bit jolly. He was named for the lion, but he looked and acted more like a bear, or a bull, though fatter than either. All he cared about in this world was private aviation, the Lord knows why. Relatives from outside subscribed him to aviation magazines, which he read at all hours of the day and night. When a plane would pass over the monastery while Brother Leo was in the courtyard, he would shade his eyes with a massive pudgy hand and gaze up at the sky as though Christ Himself were up there on a cloud. And then, like as not, tell you what sort of plane it had been. "Boeing," he'd say. "Seven oh seven." What sort of response can you make to a thing like that?

Now Brother Leo put down his magazine on the reception desk and peered at me through the top half of his bifocals. "The Sunday *Times*," he said.

"That's right," I agreed. My weekly journey on Saturday evening to get the Sunday *Times* afforded me a pleasure even Brother Leo's sour disposition couldn't spoil. It—along with Sunday Mass, of course—was the highlight of my week.

"Brother Benedict," he said, "there's something worldly about you."

I looked pointedly at his magazine, but said nothing. Having just come from confession, my soul as clean and well scrubbed as a sheet on a line, I had no desire to get into an altercation in which I might become uncharitable.

Brother Leo opened the side drawer of the desk, took out the petty cash box, and placed it atop his magazine. Opening it, he scrunched among the crumbled dollar bills toward the change at the bottom, and finally came up with two quarters and a dime. He extended his hand to me, the quarters looking like nickels in his huge palm, the dime a mere dot, and I took them, saying, "Thank you, Brother. See you in a very few minutes."

He grunted and returned to his magazine, and I went off for my weekly adventure in the outside world.

I have not always, of course, been Brother Benedict of the Crispinite Order of the Novum Mundum. In point of fact, for most of my life I wasn't even a Roman Catholic.

I was born, thirty-four years ago, to a family named Rowbottom, and was christened Charles, after a maternal grandfather. My parents having divorced in my youth, my mother next married a gentleman called Finchworthy, whose name I then used for a while. Mr. Finchworthy died in an automobile crash while I was still in high school, and my mother for some reason I never entirely understood reverted to her maiden name, Swellingsburg, taking me with her. She and I had a falling out while I was in college, so I switched back to Rowbottom, under which name I was drafted into the Army. It was simplest to keep that name even after my mother and I settled our differences, so Charles Rowbottom I remained from then until I entered the monastery.

So much for my name. (They never leave enough room on application blanks.) As to my becoming Brother Benedict, that all began in my twenty-fourth year, when I met a young lady named Anne Wilmer, a devout Roman Catholic. We fell in love, I proposed marriage and was accepted, and at her urging I undertook instruction to enter her faith. I found Roman Catholicism endlessly fascinating, as arcane and tricky and at times unfathomable as the crossword puzzle in the Sunday *Times*; and when my mother passed on shortly before I was to be baptized, my new religion was a great source of solace and comfort to me.

It was also a great source of solace and comfort a short while later, when Anne Wilmer up and ran off with a Lebanese. A practicing Mohammedan. "As a jewel of gold in a swine's snout, so is a fair woman which is without discretion." Proverbs, XI, 22. Or, as Freud put it, "What does a woman want?"

I suppose it would be fair to say I entered the monastery on the rebound from Anne Wilmer, but that wasn't the reason I stayed. I had always found the world contradictory and annoying, with no coherent place in it for me. Politically I disagreed equally with Left, Right and Center. I had no strong career goals, and my slight build and college education had left me little to look forward to but a lifetime spent somehow in the service of pieces of paper as a clerk or examiner, an administrator or counselor or staff member. Money was unimportant to me, so long as I was adequately fed and clothed and housed, and I saw no way that I was likely to attain fame or honor or any of the other talismans of worldly success. I was merely Charles Rowbottom, adrift in a white-collar sea of mundane purposelessness, and if Anne Wilmer had ditched me at any other time in my life I would surely have reacted like any of my ten million lookalikes; I would have been unhappy for a month or two, and then found an Anne Wilmer lookalike, and gone ahead with the marriage as originally planned.

˟ the timing was perfect. I had just completed my instructions in ⁺holicism, and my mind was full of religious repose. Father Dilra, ʰe priest who had been my instructor, was connected with the Cₗ ꞌinite Order, so I already knew something about it, and when I in⸜ ꞌᵢgated further it began to seem more and more that the Order oᵣ ⸜ ꞇrispin was the perfect solution to the problem of my existence.

St. Crispin and his brother St. Crispinian are the patron saints of shoemakers. In the third century the two brothers, members of a noble Roman family, traveled to Soissons where they supported themselves as shoemakers while converting many heathens to Mother Church. The emperor Maximianus (also known as Herculius) had their heads cut off around the year 286, and they were buried at Soissons. Six centuries later they were dug up again—or at any rate *somebody* was dug up— and transferred partly to Osnabruck and partly to Rome. Whether all the parts of each brother are in the same place or not is anybody's guess.

The Crispinite Order of the Novum Mundum was begun in New York City in 1777 by Israel Zapatero, a half-Moorish Spanish Jew who had converted to Catholicism solely to get himself and his worldly goods safely out of Spain so he could emigrate to America, but who then underwent a miracle in mid-ocean, a vision in which Saints Crispin and Crispinian appeared to him and told him the Church had saved his life and goods so that both could be turned to the greater glory of God. His name meaning "shoemaker" in Spanish, it was the shoemaker brothers who had been dispatched to give him his instructions. He was to found a monastic order on Manhattan Island, devoted to contemplation and good works and meditation on the meaning of Earthly travel. (Crispin and Crispinian had traveled to the scene of their missionary work, and their remains had traveled again several centuries after their deaths; Israel Zapatero was at the moment of his miracle traveling; and the very concept of shoes implies travel.)

Thus, upon arrival in New York, Zapatero took a ninety-nine-year lease on a bit of land north of the main part of Manhattan, assembled some monks from somewhere, and built a monastery. The Order sputtered along, supported by Zapatero and by begging, but never had more than half a dozen monks in residence until the Civil War, when a sudden upsurge in vocations occurred. Just after the turn of the century there was a schism, and a dissident faction went off to found the Crispinianite Order in South Brooklyn, but that by-blow faded away long since, while the original Order has continued to prosper, within its limitations.

The limitations are many. We are still within the confines of the one original monastery, with no intention or hope of ever expanding. We are neither a teaching nor a missionary Order, and so are little heard of in the outside world. We are a contemplative

Order, concerning ourselves with thoughts of God and Travel. There are at the moment sixteen of us, housed in the original Spanish-Moorish-Colonial-Greek-Hebraic building put up by Israel Zapatero nearly two centuries ago, which has room for only twenty residents at the most. Our meditations on Travel have so far produced the one firm conclusion that Travel should never be undertaken lightly, and only when absolutely necessary to the furthering of the glory of God among men—which means we rarely go anywhere.

All of which suits me admirably. I prefer not to be part of a large sprawling hierarchical organization, some monkish Pentagon somewhere, but feel more comfortable with the casual comradeship possible among sixteen mild-mannered men sharing the same roof. I also like the monastery building itself, its tumbled-together conglomeration of styles, the dark warmth of the chestnut woodwork everywhere within, the intricate carving in the chapel and refectory and offices, the tile mosaic floors, the arched ceilings, the gray stone block exterior: the whole giving the effect of a California Spanish mission and a medieval English monastery intermingled in the mind of Cecil B. DeMille.

As to Travel, I never did care much for that. I am perfectly willing to spend the rest of my life within the monastery walls as Brother Benedict, now and forever.

Except, of course, for my weekly sally to Lexington Avenue for the Sunday *Times*…